THE END IS NEAR

CONNOR MCCARTEN

The End is Near

TABLE OF CONTENTS

ABOUT THE AUTHOR 5

COPYRIGHT 6

CHAPTER ONE 9

CHAPTER TWO 35

CHAPTER THREE 69

CHAPTER FOUR 85

CHAPTER FIVE 109

CHAPTER SIX 133

CHAPTER SEVEN 161

CHAPTER EIGHT 195

CHAPTER NINE 223

CHAPTER TEN 247

CHAPTER ELEVEN 267

ACKNOWLEDGEMENTS 273

The End is Near

ABOUT THE AUTHOR

Connor McCarten was born and lives in Liverpool, a Law graduate of the University of Liverpool. This is Connor McCarten's debut novel as a fiction author.

COPYRIGHT

This is a work of fiction. Names, characters, organisations, places, events, incidents are either products of the author's imagination or are used fictitiously. Any resemblance to actual persons, living or dead, or actual events is purely coincidental.

Text copyright © 2025 belongs to Connor McCarten.

The moral right of Connor McCarten to be identified as the author of this work has been asserted in accordance with the Copyright, Designs and Patents Act 1988. All rights reserved.

First published in Great Britain in 2025 by Amazon.

The End is Near

No part of this book may be reproduced, or stored in a retrieval system, or transmitted in any form or by any means, electronic, mechanical, photocopying, reading, or otherwise, without express written permission of the author and publisher.

Every effort has been made to obtain the necessary permissions with reference to copyright material, both illustrative and quoted. We apologise for any omissions in this respect and will be pleased to make the appropriate acknowledgements in any future edition.

Published by Amazon. Amazon and the Amazon logo are trademarks of Amazon.com Inc., or its affiliates.

Cover art by Ailsa Ogden Studio (@ailsaogden.studio)

The End is Near

CHAPTER ONE

As the months approached mid-October in the English port city of Liverpool, the temperature had continued to deteriorate to frosty conditions. The wind grew more fierce, the leaves eroded to darker colours of brown, and there was an icy climate typical for British weather in late autumn. The pale sunlight penetrated the rectangular window of their compact first-storey bedroom flat, a room that often felt like a prison cell because of its miserable furnishings and musty smell – the only time it felt cosy being when asleep.

Taylor's eyes fluttered open at the illumination steadying in from outside, taking a moment to absorb the natural autumnal sunlight before he turned over to read the time, his exhausted body instantaneously fuelled with frustration. The digital alarm clock read 08:58 a.m. in bold numbers. He audibly grunted at the realisation that he had slept in past his alarm, again – an act not out of the ordinary, in fact, his sleeping pattern had deteriorated to that of an insomniac, which meant late bedtimes and even later mornings – and was already an hour late for work.

He climbed out of bed with as much effort as possible, glancing over at his partner Callum still in a deep sleep. He stumbled over a can of beer on his way to the bathroom and noted the previous night's escapades scattered across the bedroom floor. Discarded cans of beer, cigarette butts, and drug paraphernalia in the form of empty bags, a single crumpled note, and a plastic straw. The equipment lay dormant and made Taylor hazily reminisce on the attempted euphoria from the previous night, which seemed to be nothing more than a muffled memory.

Staring back at his expression in the stained bathroom mirror, he examined the shoddy change to his profile: a manmade consequence of his lifestyle choices. Dark eyes; dried saliva around his bloodstained lips from excessive biting; cracks in his forehead; decayed incisors that needed urgently removing, he had complained consistently about toothache for over a month, but had been removed from his dentist registry for failing to attend any scheduled routine checkups. Although Taylor looked bad, he never cared, because he thought he was still more handsome than the average person. The monotony of his routine paired with a comedown from excessive drug use made the concept of living and working a gruelling chore. He closed his eyes and thought of how life would eventually change for the better; how this life that he had lived for the past 28 years would soon be a thing of the past; nothing more than a chapter in his autobiography saturated with grief.

The End is Near

He observed his surroundings – the grimy white tiles on the walls stained yellow from nicotine; the mould in the grout of the tiles; the dirty shower curtain that housed billions of particles of bacteria; the floral green curtain that covered the mini rectangular window, hung in the bathroom since the previous occupants that neither could afford to change. He sometimes felt like a maniac living in a psychiatric unit with no way of escaping rather than in the surroundings of his own loving home. His environment had made him more lethargic than anticipated but he never had the effort or financial capacity to alter its interior design.

Taylor had opened the bathroom cabinet and decided on two codeine to aid his throbbing head because ordinary painkillers would not assist the ache in his body. He washed his face with the miniscule remains of a bar of soap – that needed to be peeled from the mouldy basin – deep within the crevices of his pores. This was followed by drying his face with the only available towel at the end of the bath. The towel was damp and stained with a crimson liquid he knew was blood. Blood was also stained on the edge of the bath that had descended down onto the grey tiles of the bathroom floor. It was bright red meaning it was relatively fresh, and thoughts began to run through Taylor's mind about the night prior. He had to stop himself from thinking of what had occurred in order to get ready for work, already late.

He opened his bedside table and took out black socks and cheap boxer shorts that had a hole at the waistband, and headed towards the lonely oak wardrobe based in the right corner of the small square bedroom. He took out the only polo shirt visible, jeans, and Adidas trainers that he wore solely for the purposes of work. He rapidly dressed within five minutes – carefully observing the peaceful expression on Callum's sleepy face – and exited the bedroom, out of the flat, and down the stairs in the block, with a slight jog to make it to the bus stop on time.

He pulled out his mobile phone and called the first person listed in his contacts. His boss, Adrian. It was the third time within the span of five working days that he had been late. He had blamed his alarm, sickness, and forgetfulness regarding his start time. He wondered what excuse he could make next.

'Hey, Ade… sorry… sorry, yeah – I slept in. I will be about 15 minutes. Yeah, I'm sorry. Sorry. I know, it won't happen again… *no*. No party, I had a rough night of sleep. Callum was up all night – sick. Thanks mate, I won't be long. Bye,' Taylor said robotically through the phone. He ended the call and breathed a sigh of relief, searching through his jeans pocket until he found his tangled earphones.

His phone had 38 missed calls over the past three days and multiple texts from local drug dealers, threatening to end his life for unpaid cocaine debts that had now accrued interest for late repayment. He clicked on the first text message from a dealer named Robbie and the instant dread crept in. Robbie Barton lived within a two-mile radius of Taylor's flat and terrified most people beyond comprehension. He was 37 years old with thick brown hair and a large red scar on his left cheek from being involved in a knife fight with another local gang. Robbie was infamously known throughout Liverpool for being a criminal gang leader.

'Do *not* get on the wrong side of that bastard, for your own sake. He's nuts,' Taylor had remembered his father mentioning when he spotted the two standing together sharing a spliff. Robbie had also recently been released from prison, serving 9 years' imprisonment for stabbing an innocent bystander and his girlfriend during a brawl in the city centre.

Taylor toyed ways on how to produce the debts plus interest as soon as possible. His parents had already borrowed him too much cash and was therefore afraid to arouse any further suspicions from them, his bank account was £456 overdrawn, and his credit score was beyond resurrection in order to obtain a payday loan to settle debts to an underground kingpin.

ANSWER THE FONE

U R DEAD BELIEVE ME

I WANT MY MONEY ASAP. I WILL NEVER DO U A FAVOUR EVER AGAIN

Taylor reread the messages three times, and then quickly locked the screen of his phone and slid it back into his pocket. Out of sight, out of mind. Another dealer had been crossed off the list. No more favours; no more coke on tick; no more ease of access to the substance craved the most.

Taylor's mind distanced to Callum and how he wished that it had been somebody else – a foreign entity he had never met – sharing a bed with him. Instant fury began to explode through his brain, just as it always did when he thought about Callum's timid, obsessive demeanour. Taylor thought of how needy Callum was. He loathed his presence, often daydreaming of abandoning him without an explanation. Although he wished for the strength to discard every trace of Callum's mere existence from his life, he knew that he could never do it. The reasons why he could not discard of him were unknown: hidden deep within his subconscious brain, unable to access.

He watched the local suburban area disintegrate before him from the bus window: in a trance, thinking about the first time that he had ever met Callum.

They had met 15 months ago at a local bar, The Red Horses, more commonly known without the colour in its name. Known throughout the entirety of the urban area of Liverpool for being a council estate meeting point filled with drug-fuelled creatures – the vast majority were youth from low-income housing – that needed to be avoided. It looked more like a neighbourhood community centre than a bar, standing opposite a row of three-bed terraced council houses. The bar was bare brick on the exterior, except for a broken sign on the right that read "THE RED HORE" (the two S' had been ripped down by local yobs to act as an "anagram" for whore – although the incorrect spelling). Metal bars were attached to the small square windows at the front, with a miniscule smoking area nestled at the back that was invisible to the naked eye until you entered the establishment and followed the fire exit signs to the rear.

Knife fights; cheap alcohol; drugs; indoor smoking; young girls in their early teens being groped by men in their late 20s. Taylor was one of The Horses' best customers and had spent years of his adolescent life there, from the age of 13 when he had become friends with people double his age and decided that rebelling against his parents was paramount to gain respect amongst his peers.

The interior of the bar was archaically decorated, not refurbished since it opened in 1986, with peel and stick flooring housing billions of bacteria cells. A large wooden bar was opposite the entrance, covering most of the floor except for small seating areas to the left – by the toilets – and right. The seats were upholstered in a tacky floral print typical throughout pubs in the 70s and 80s, and a professional germophobe would be terrified by the state of the premises. Damp, chipped woodwork, toilets that permanently stunk of urine, discarded cigarette butts and joints stuck to the uncleaned floors.

The humidity of July '22's weather was the most oppressive Liverpool had seen in over 35 years according to the Met Office. Flocks of people from around the country had migrated to Liverpool for the day to arrive at its beaches. Happy faces, children as young as five playing on their iPhones, shirtless men, women with the cheeks of their derrière on full display. It seemed to Taylor as though every person had journeyed to Liverpool for a taste of saltwater.

The 15th of July was a hopeful new chapter in Taylor's life who had just got the keys to his own flat, sourced by his adult social worker. The relationship at home with his parents had become strained since his grandfather had died the year prior and his father's alcoholism had taken a toll on family life. Gambling debts, heated arguments, and physical abuse against his mother. The local authority had been informed of shouting coming from the family home which resulted in Taylor forming a bond with Jeannette. He made up lies regarding the brawls at home because he knew that if he lied, he would be more likely to get on the property ladder quicker.

'If others can swindle the government, why can't I?' Taylor often asked himself. Becoming a high risk individual for government housing was a blessing to Taylor, who struggled to avoid an overdraft every month due to excessive spending on booze, cigarettes, cannabis, and cocaine. Therefore, affording his own property without governmental support seemed an impossibility.

When he received the call from Jeannette that their bid had been accepted for a one-bedroom flat two miles away from his childhood home, he remembered the excitement he felt that bordered on an experience of joy.

'I can't believe it. I'm officially a homeowner… I couldn't have done this without you, Jeannette. Thank you,' he had muttered over the phone when she told him of the good news.

Wednesday was a time for celebration, which had brought Taylor to The Horses with his longest friend of 26 years, Stacey. Stacey was an enigma, a peculiar mixed race being with thick black hair always sleek in a tight bun that sculpted her face flawlessly. She had a wire figure and bulging dark eyes that housed the potential to become a model. Stacey bear no other friends except for Taylor which made her hard to understand and confused as being intimidating, shallow, and antisocial.

'Is that the one who has always got them big, massive headphones across her head?' – 'Yeah, I know her. The only black on the estate.' – 'She's strange. Always alone. She's probably never had a dick in her life.'

Taylor loved that Stacey was mysterious to everybody except her parents and himself, who knew her as low maintenance, goofy and outgoing.

'Don't have me out until all hours, Tay. Some of us cannot function in work with a hangover. No drugs either, please. Let's just have a couple of drinks to celebrate you,' Stacey had said. However, Taylor had already agreed for drugs to be dropped off at six o'clock. As his night was classified as a special occasion – he had purchased two grams of coke, a gram of ketamine, and two ecstasy pills to reward himself.

Taylor boasted to mixed emotions about his recent property development – 'Well done, Tay, the parties are in yours then.' – 'Fuck, all I need is a few mental issues to get out of my mum's then.' – 'Just ignore Ronnie. He's a miserable, jealous bastard. Well done, kidder.' – but his state of euphoria was unmatched. The cocaine had begun to travel through his bloodstream and he felt ready to party. The unavailability of natural daylight within The Horses made it feel like an underground speakeasy. A place where people congregated to forget the disparities of the outside world, where people collided on the dancefloor to forget their troubles, where Taylor felt free of judgement away from those who never understood him.

The heat had brought strangers into The Horses – a service station for people descending home from the local beach and forests to the further suburban areas. The establishment was at peak capacity, with the temperature inside the bar more humid than the hot summer sun outside. Beautiful men and women of all shapes, sizes, races, and genders surrounded Taylor. The erotic feeling of cocaine pulsing through his blood made him understand the beauty that every person possessed, which was different from his usual judgemental personality. Broken noses; open pores; sunken eyes; curvaceous figures.

There was a stranger across the bar who had matched his gaze with a reciprocated stare. A fair-skinned male who looked no older than 18 stood with a lovestruck expression spread across his face. Taylor realised that whoever the stranger was, was attractive, with thick brown hair combed over across his forehead, a tiny petite figure that made his vest hang awkwardly across his body, and skinny ripped jeans that highlighted pale legs with no hair on them. Taylor continued his conversation with Stacey and Mac, another local, but could still feel the stranger's watchful eyes observing his every move. Watching how Taylor tipped his pint glass back to retrieve all of the liquid down his throat; the veins raised on the back of his hands from heavy lifting at work; the way his facial hair grew thinner the closer it got to his sideburns.

The End is Near

The music intensified the later it got, and Taylor had shifted his drug of choice from cocaine to ketamine. Ketamine had a dissociative effect on Taylor's body, with hallucinations often occurring. He felt like doing nothing but dancing when he snorted ketamine, and a night of celebratory dancing was how he intended to commemorate the news. Stacey had left, citing anxiety over the growing crowd, which meant Taylor was free to diverse his time however he pleased.

He made his way from the bar and into the only cubicle in the men's bathroom. He opened the zippy bag filled with ketamine and poured a stack of white powder all over the crease of his thumb, absorbing every shard through his left nostril. He felt the instant burning sensation to the ring of his nostril and buried his face within his hand again, ensuring every crumb of powder was inhaled; pounding larger crumbs down to digest efficiently. He emptied more of the bag onto his hand, and snorted another pile. Empty. Snort. Empty. Snort. As he inhaled the shards of white powder, he felt the difference in texture compared to that of cocaine. Ketamine had a sharp feeling against the nostrils and an almost instantaneous effect on the body. He closed the bag abruptly and slid it back into his pocket, unlocked the cubicle door, and made his way out of the gentlemen's.

As Taylor exited the tiny cubicle, he noticed the young fella who had been slowly falling in love with him from across the bar had followed him; standing with his arms crossed and back rested comfortably against the wall. He vacantly stared at him, presumably waiting for some form of conversation. As Taylor stood and observed the stranger, he noticed that his skin was so pale that it looked as though he was glistening in the overhead lighting. He had perfect blemish free skin and rosy lips. Taylor could see the outline of his chest against the white vest, with rounded nipples that rubbed against the cotton as his body moved unknowingly.

'What are you looking at me like that for?' Taylor asked gingerly.

'I could hear you in there. *Naughty*. That stuff is no good for you, you do know that?' the stranger remarked with an eery expression on his face. An expression Taylor could not figure out, but on retrospective thinking, it seemed like worry.

'Yeah? And what are you? A shrink?' Taylor laughed, wiping around the rim of his nostril.

'Nope, not at all. Just a normal lad who likes a drink.'

'Jeans on in this weather? You must be a vampire. I've never seen you in here before. What's your name?'

'I always have jeans on. And I didn't know that you owned this place to know every person who walks through the door… my name is Callum. What's your name?'

'You are cheeky. My name is Taylor, nice to meet you. Fancy a drink?' Taylor asked.

'I would love one, thanks.' Callum pulled himself down from the sink that he had been resting on, making sure to fix his long brown hair in the mirror and checking his complexion for any non-existent blemishes.

As they left the toilet, Taylor placed his hand on Callum's waist and they made their way through the thick of the crowd towards the bar, feeling the heat of Callum's skin underneath the texture of his denim skinny jeans, who caressed the top of Taylor's hand as they manoeuvred their way further into the pit of business. Callum observed Taylor's interactions with everyone and wondered how somebody so obscure could be so popular amongst his peers. He timidly ushered his way through the crowd, following his master's lead, politely smiling at everyone he passed. He turned his head to where he had stood previously and noticed that his only friend Emma had left without any announcement. He had took his phone out of his jeans pocket to ask for her whereabouts – interrupted by Taylor asking what he wanted to drink – but unfortunately forgot, which was the start of the end of their friendship.

'Shall we dance?' Taylor shouted in his ear, and pulled Callum by the arm through the hectic crowd to the undesignated dancefloor – an empty vessel in the centre of the bar that people had no option but to avoid as people's arms floated around in ecstasy. A disco song from the 1980s played, the beat intensifying the closer they got to the surround sound speakers. Callum lifted his arms in the air and spun his head around, failing to remember the last time he had that much fun carelessly dancing. Taylor placed his large hands on Callum's petite waist and moved side to side to the thudding beat of the music. In that electric moment, neither cared about their surroundings or their bizarre dance moves that lacked rhythm.

After a while, Taylor grabbed Callum's hand and they shuffled their way to the hidden smoking area. The time was past ten p.m. and the humidity outside was still deadly. There were around ten people in the desolate smoking area, all lined on the metal zig-zag benches smoking and jesting.

A girl – who looked around mid-twenties – sat alone in the corner of the smoking area taking exaggerated drags of a cigarette. Callum had noticed her ethereal beauty; the glossy texture of her rosy cheeks and thin eyebrows that made her look doll-like. She had a black linen skirt on with a vest top that highlighted her erect pink nipples – the left was pierced – and coral Adidas shoes with yellow stripes across the side. Callum struggled to concentrate on Taylor or his presence for a short while as he continued to stare at the girl in the corner. Wondering who she was, why she was alone, and whether she knew how beautiful she was.

'Who is that girl?' Callum asked, interrupting Taylor who had been mumbling about nothing of importance for a while.

'No idea. Never saw her before. Why?' Taylor said. He offered his joint to Callum who politely declined.

'No reason why. I just thought that she is beautiful. Her skin is perfect.'

After a couple of seconds of silence, Taylor asked a question that seemed rhetoric in nature. 'Are you gay?' He received a response in the form of laughter. 'I will take that as a yes then.'

'I'm 100% gay. I don't fancy her, if that is what you thought I meant. I just think she is beautiful. Her lips are a beautiful shape, as you can see when she takes a pull on her cigarette. I don't know… I just find her mysterious for some reason, just the way she is sat all alone and seems so nonchalant… I probably sound a bit weird, examining people like this, sorry. I just love to people-watch,' Callum said.

'I agree with you, I suppose. She is a pretty girl, but I think that she knows it.' Callum raised an eyebrow for Taylor to elaborate on his bold statement. 'She is sat alone in the smoking area of a crowded bar surrounded by probably one hundred men inside, yet she has chosen to sit outside on her own and has not made eye contact with anyone. To see if anyone is looking at her. To acknowledge anyone. Nothing. That to me is confidence mixed with vanity.'

Callum pondered on Taylor's opinion and noted the truth in his words. Callum was very timid and would never sit alone without sweat soaking through his clothing at the thought of a human looking at him for longer than half a second.

'So, I wanted to ask if you had a boyfriend?' Taylor asked after a while.

'I don't. Do you have a… girlfriend?' Callum asked politely.

'Fella or bird, either-or. I'm bisexual, mate. Everyone knows it, too. But no, single. Could not be bothered being in a relationship.'

'How come? Do you never want a partner?'

'At this point, I'll say no. Headache after headache. Arguing. People unable to keep it in their pants. The thought makes me queasy,' Taylor said, discarding the end of his joint on the floor. Multiple ashtrays being within a two-step walking distance had irritated Callum, who hated people who chose to litter. He believed that small acts of littering were the main catalysts in global warming as they were the most socially acceptable acts often overlooked.

As the volume of the music stayed at an intense rate, Taylor and Callum continued to dance for what felt like forever, until the manager Tony had killed the music and shouted loudly for everyone to disperse outside. Around 40 people left simultaneously with Taylor and Callum, after Taylor had said his goodbyes to Tony.

Stars twinkled in the night sky, making sweat particles glisten on everybody's foreheads. They stood close – with Taylor's hands tucked into the waistband of Callum's tight jeans – and Callum struggled to decipher whether it was the humidity or proximity of their bodies that had inclined the heat. The two of them together shared some semblance of normalcy to bystanders – people had automatically assumed they were together – but it was abnormal for the pair as Callum had never had more than a one-night stand with a partner, and Taylor had only ever had one serious relationship when he was 17 and that was with a woman.

Her name was Talia and she was 26 years of age, now a distant memory to Taylor who much preferred sex with men. They had met when Taylor sold Talia some weed for a friend – he was a puritan about selling drugs at that age but agreed to assist his friend on that one occasion because he had been informed that Talia was "easy enough" to have sex with – and within two hours of instant chat messaging they had sex whilst her nine-month-old infant was asleep upstairs and the child's father was in jail for drug charges.

'Do you fancy coming back to mine for a quick drink? We could get a taxi… or we could even walk. It would take us about 40 minutes though,' Taylor asked Callum.

'I'd like that. Yes, let's walk. You lead the way.'

On their expedition to the flat, Taylor felt embarrassed about somebody other than just himself seeing the flat for the first time in the likely event it was disorderly. The pair stopped at the only 24/7 garage in a three mile radius that consisted of a haul of two bottles of cheap rosé wine and a share bag of cheese and onion crisps. Callum wondered why Taylor chose to buy cheese and onion when the risk of bad breath was palpable.

They talked about Taylor's career at a wholesale warehouse he had worked at since age 25, his desire to become the general manager one day, Callum's part-time work at a care home over the water whilst he was studying Sociology at university, Taylor's new flat, Callum's living arrangements in the south of Liverpool with his grandmother, and the fear of hate crimes in the city centre against openly queer men that only Callum felt.

They headed up the stairs and into the flat. Callum surveyed the somewhat blank canvas with a standardised basic grey carpet that ran through the entirety of the flat except the kitchen and bathroom. The ceiling was filthy with large stains of mould and grime throughout, an exhausting view for both of them. Taylor was appalled when he saw the state of the living room and wondered to himself how he would ever be able to call this place home. They both observed the mess before them; a large brown leather sofa with cigarette burns sat in the middle of the room that looked like the poster for a horror movie; red, white, and black paint was splattered across the walls with grey floral wallpaper peeling off one wall; the thick smell of damp lingered in the air; ash and cigarette butts were stuck to the windowsill. There was an archaic electric fireplace nestled in the alcove of the living room with a large dent in, clearly made by a foot.

'The last people here have clearly left it as a dump. I'm going to make it my own though: homely. I've decided how I want to furnish it.' Taylor made up plans for decorating with theatrical hands floating around the living room. Mentioning where he wanted wooden shelves hung, a TV on a glass stand, a dining table in the corner, and brown curtains to match the wallpaper.

Callum watched in awe as Taylor strolled around the room discussing what fixtures and fittings he wanted and where they would go, and thought about his own future and the hope that his future residence would be so proudly thought out. He nodded along to Taylor's ideas and noticed his whole demeanour changing the more that he spoke – a sign that the drugs were wearing off.

The End is Near

After conversing about nothing in particular; Taylor drank half of one of the bottles of cheap rosé, passing the bottle to Callum once finished. He planted himself down onto the sofa that squeaked terribly once any pressure was applied to it: a sign of its usage. Callum sat on the edge of the sofa, as far away from Taylor as possible, and took small sips of wine. The £6 price tag was obvious because of the pungent vinegar smell emanating from the bottle and the faces both of them pulled struggling to swallow it down. He passed the bottle back to Taylor as they sat in silence, exchanging the bottle between one another, the taste easing as Callum's throat became accustomed to the miserable flavour of the wine.

Taylor felt in his pocket for his supply of drugs and scooped another mountain of lumpy white cocaine onto his palm as Callum sat and observed the veins protruding at the side of his neck. A thought came into his mind whether the veins would protrude when Taylor was on top of a man or woman in bed, but decided to suppress the thought quickly. He wondered whether he should make conversation about Taylor's life, his parents, or why he took drugs, but decided against it. He hated the idea of becoming too intrusive with a stranger he only knew the first name of. He thought again, maybe to ask what he had in mind to do with the flat, but then realised this conversation had already been done.

Callum looked down at his palms which were wet and clammy from anxiety. He continued to anticipate Taylor beginning a deep conversation, discussing past and future plans and dreams, but stopped every time

Taylor continued to drink from the bottle and ignore his presence. He wondered Taylor's intentions for inviting him to the flat when he could have sat alone. However, Callum peculiarly thought that maybe his presence alone was enough for Taylor to feel content. He sat and smiled at the thought of his presence being enough but then backtracked. Taylor would likely be using him out of boredom, convenience, or pity, and no positive thought about being a good person could change the reality.

Callum was easily manipulated and always had been since a young age. He possessed low self-esteem and his awkward traits in social settings made him easy bait for people with their own personal vendettas, or men who wanted to get laid. He knew his lack of confidence was caused by childhood trauma; treating it seemed impossible. He wasn't unhappy per se but he had a lot of work to do on himself. Counselling as a child had failed him, anti-depressants never touched the sides, a life filled with loving family and friends did him no further favours, nor did a sheltered life when he detoxed himself from society for a couple of long days.

As Taylor continued to take drugs, Callum's mind trailed back to an article that he had read during one of his sleepless nights when he wanted to build research on his *Family Life in a Working Class Society* module at university and the effects of Class A substances on the body. He often wondered at what point of the night did an individual begin to think that they needed a bag of cocaine to survive the supposed fun. Could people who drank alcohol regularly drink without drugs? Or was the drug taking an essential in order to function in a social setting? Surely the after effects of drugs outweighed the prospect of a night on them, Callum thought to himself. The feeling of anxiety; suicide; depression; regret; guilt. The desire to do nothing except sit in bed and cry, contemplating life, and what the meaning to anything was. For Callum, drugs seemed to cause an inability to see the beauty of the little things in life.

After a slim duration of silence, Callum had decided that he wanted to leave the flat and return back home – home being £35 away in a taxi, and no buses able to take him until at least half five in the morning.

'God, I really don't know how I am going to get home. My phone is dead, you don't have a charger, and I have about £5 left. I don't have my card, either. Wow, I'm a nightmare. I really want to head home soon, though. The wine is nearly gone and I am getting *so* tired,' he did a fake yawn to emphasise his lethargy.

'We got two bottles, remember? This is only the first. Okay, if you want to go, you can do. Ummm, why don't you stay? You live far away, don't you? It will cost you a fortune in a taxi. I don't have my bed yet so we would have to sleep on this dirty old sofa but sure we could make that work.' On further thinking, Taylor said, 'or I could sleep on the floor – if that is any easier for you?'

'I suppose I could stay for a little while longer, thanks. Saving me a lot of money in a taxi.'

To show his appreciation for Callum's resistance to going home, Taylor raised the volume of the music on his phone and stood Callum up to dance around the living room under the dim lightbulb above them. They eventually kissed and Callum could feel the sparks between them; imaginary fireworks exploding outside on the council estate. In juxtaposition, the only feeling that Taylor felt was the dying need for sexual intercourse.

As they continued to kiss, Taylor removed his top, revealing a defined chest with thick hairs that grew downwards from his chest to his belly button. Callum continued to marvel at the sight before him with a sense of lust, Taylor dropping his shorts to the floor, revealing a heavy erection protruding through his loose boxers.

Callum allowed his jeans to drop to the ground, leaving his slim childlike stature to be exposed, wearing nothing but tight black briefs and ankle socks, erect pink nipples poking from his chest. Callum ran his hand through Taylor's brown hair, moaning when he felt his teeth plucked against his nipple like he imagined a new born would on its mother's breast for feeding time. Taylor slid his wet fingers slowly inside of him and felt the insides of his hole rubbing against his broad fingers.

'You feel so good, you're so tight.'

'Fuck me now. *Please*,' Callum begged, already on the verge of climaxing.

'Get on your knees first,' Taylor ordered. After performing fellatio, Callum mounted himself onto the sofa and buried his face in the crusty leather of the sofa; disgusted by the thought of potential unspeakable things happening where his face calmly rested.

Taylor massaged his saliva onto the tip of his penis, sliding inside of Callum's hole who felt the painful tinge of penetration ascending from his rectum up to his spine. When he felt as far inside as possible, Taylor thrust rapidly until he ejaculated with euphoria.

'Did you like that?' Taylor asked as he pulled his underwear back on.

'I loved it. Would it still be okay if I stay over?'

'Of course. I offered for you to stay,' Taylor said. Callum put on his briefs and they both lay dormant on the sofa. Ready for sleep. The moon stood high in the sky as the night settled in until they both fell asleep.

Their thoughts ran parallel. One of hope for the distant future, the other of pleasure of the recent past. That night was the most intimate that Callum had ever been with a man. He had never slept on the sofa with anyone, or danced with a man in his own home, or passed a bottle of wine back and forth with one singular person. Taylor had changed his perception of men and he hoped that it would be the first night of something special.

CHAPTER TWO

Taylor arrived at work less than half an hour after he had woken up; his brain flooded with memories of the first time him and Callum met. Milton's was a wholesalers located on an industrial park just a few miles away from Taylor's flat, open to businesses and the general public to purchase unnecessary amounts of food and drink in bulk. Whoever needed 72 cans of fizzy orange, Milton's had it. He had worked there for three years and hoped to become the store manager in the foreseeable future. But for now, he had to start a gruelling day of work wishing that he was still in bed and not the only breadwinner of the family.

The different lights – the early morning sun, headlights, traffic lights, and indoor lights reflecting from the shop window – sent overwhelming feelings through Taylor's body that his comedown struggled to handle.

Callum had been fired from his previous job at the care home since he had repeatedly missed shifts without any notice, and also managed a third in his degree at university which most prospective employers would not entertain. This meant all outgoings rested on Taylor to fund – overworked from long hours and two drug addictions to feed. The demand had slowly become too much for him to handle.

Taylor scanned his lanyard to gain access to the staffroom and was met with a stern expression from Adrian already sat down at the table waiting – arms crossed in a quite apparent hand-me-down fleece which was matted with hairs and stains. Adrian was only 33 but his maturity was otherworldly compared to Taylor's. He was five-foot seven with a scrawny build and electric ginger hair always spiked in style; his alias "The Firecracker" at Milton's. They had become friends from years of working together, which escalated to partying on weekends together and smoking weed outside on their dinner breaks.

'Morning, Adrian. Sorry about being late. It won't happen again, I promise.'

'Tay, you have been late three times out of the last five. You have used every excuse under the sun over the years. Pneumonia; sickness; some random person you have never mentioned before being dead. You must think that I was born yesterday. Listen, I know you are saying Callum's not well, but come on. You look terrible, your eyes are bloodshot, and you look like you have been dug up from the grave. I'm trying to look out for you. I know you are back on the gear. I don't care what you get up to on your days off, but coming to work looking the way you do after a heavy night is not all right. It's not the first time either, I've had your back many times to Sandeep wanting to get rid of you. You are a good worker when you want to be but this is the last time. Think of this as a formal warning. Do not fuck it up,' Adrian had asserted his dominance. Taylor could not lift his glance up from his hands when spoken to, guilt-ridden how a manager he called a friend could not rely on him; guilty for the excuses he had made; guilty for allowing Callum in his life.

'Adrian, honestly. I'm okay. I promise. Callum is sick. I'm sorry, I'll work extra time for free if I need to. I feel terrible, I never meant to be unreliable.'

'Whatever. Just forget about it now. Look after yourself, okay. That is all I want. You know there's help available out there? Have a look online. Bye, kidder.'

Afterwards, Taylor had recounted the conversation with confusion. Needing help? One thing that Taylor knew he would never need was a shrink. He liked to dabble in Class A substances from time to time, but who never? He could not think of one person under the age of 35 in his life who never recreationally experimented with drugs at the weekend. The euphoria of an ecstasy pill was something unexplainable to any human except those who had experienced the drug and knew the feeling. The erotica of the discotheque; the host of figures in an illegal rave; the love you felt for everyone and everything; the desire to party until early hours the next morning. Drugs were common in working class Liverpool, and Adrian should know that: he was one of the many regular users. Taylor had witnessed Adrian first-hand, sniffing cocaine from his kitchen counter and smoking weed during work hours.

Unpacking; loading; forklift driving; manual handling; answering customer queries. Methodically, he unpacked his loads of stock in bulk onto the shelves. He always fixed stock pedantically, his favourite being items kept individually, so he could sort every item separately with the logo facing forward, perfectly aligned with all neighbouring stock.

Taylor's thoughts trailed to Callum – again – in bed, and a tinge of anger spiralled through his insides. He loathed him for what he had brought to their relationship. Their relationship what was a mistake; a relationship out of convenience; a relationship out of pity after threats of suicide from Callum. Taylor was now slaving away – working up to 50 hours a week when his contract stipulated a maximum of 37.5 – at Milton's to ensure they had money for food; cigarettes; booze; electricity; gas. Carnage brewed inside of him whenever he thought of Callum. How much longer could he put up with their relationship? he thought to himself. Callum's laziness and depressed thoughts were getting too much.

On the right hemisphere of their coupling, Callum woke at two in the afternoon – later than anticipated – with a stinging headache, a dose of amnesia, and anger towards himself for how life was continuing to progress. He had remembered setting his alarm the previous night to wake up early; hoping to have gone for a long walk to clear his mind – he decided on getting the bus to the beach to soak up the crisp October air and listen to a true crime podcast – but failed when Taylor had arrived home with two grams of coke.

Callum detested the person that he had become. A boy once filled with ambition – that would always harbour feelings of childhood trauma – was now the epitome of failure. A failed degree, no career prospects, an addict to drugs, and in a volatile relationship being physically and mentally abused by his narcissistic partner.

As the sun attempted to glow through the thick grey clouds, he continued to reflect on his current life and the route it had taken. Drinking, drugs, likely dead or on heroin within the next couple of years. He tried to rescue a memory of his old self – before Taylor and life of constant drinking – but failed to conjure anything positive up.

Within the space of a year, he had changed from someone full of ambition to a self-depreciating menace with no care for the effects his lifestyle had on him. From being nurtured by his grandmother since the age of three with a tight-knit friendship group flooded with compliments and moral support, he now sniffed cocaine six nights a week and allowed himself to be manipulated and abused at the hands of his partner. It was impossible for Callum to remember the last time he felt truly loved, or received a warm embrace from him.

He thought of the aggressive sex they had the night prior. The lack of consent from Taylor to initiate love-making. Spitting in his face, strangulation, and calling him derogatory names whilst he lay semi-conscious was how he defined love-making. He abided by the unspoken rules put in place by Taylor – to always agree with his recommendations, to never argue against his decisions, to remain as submissive as humanly possible. Callum must not have any input on the workings of their relationship for it to function.

Callum's thoughts travelled to his grandmother, who had supported him since birth – becoming his full-time legal guardian from age three – and his repayment to her. She would be disgraced at the trajectory of her baby's life. The lack of aspiration, education, wages, love, and health. The countless times she had turned down a job promotion at the knicker factory; cancelling evenings out with her friends; struggling to pay the bills; struggling with her own sanity at 60 years of age, being the primary caregiver for a toddler she never wanted.

The worst part of his day was having to look in the mirror, his reflection showing an alien entity he never knew. Sunken and bloodshot eyes that were once inviting and full of life; tangled hair stuck to his head; a limp body skinnier than ever before, revealing his rib cage through his pale white skin. Beyond the physical reflection, all that Callum saw was a lifeless soul.

He noted the love bites descending down from his chin to his nipples, marks of Taylor's dominance across his body that he never consented to. He hated the bites, but Taylor never cared for his opinion. 'It's how I leave my mark on you, so everybody knows that you are *mine*.' But nobody else ever saw Callum shirtless.

Happiness was no longer a feeling within Callum's emotional catalogue – everything felt like a passing ship. A passing ship that he saw through binoculars from a deserted island 2,000 miles away. Sex was no longer love-making, it was a time to lie and take whatever Taylor had planned, which meant painful, aggressive sex. Exercising was a chore he never possessed the energy for. Reading was no longer a love, it exhausted him. His imagination had ceased to exist. He despised doing anything, besides doing nothing.

Callum made no effort to look after himself because he was prisoner within their flat. His once luscious head of hair was now greasy and knotted; the evidence of not visiting the barber for over six months apparent, his hair broad and solid, desperation for nutrients apparent from every strand. The man in the mirror was not him anymore. It was an illusion: a creature that had taken on a new life form.

The End is Near

Failing to wake up early every morning to fix his life was a daily ritual. The days rolled into one – he had no idea whether it was a Monday or a Saturday – and weeks rolled into months, and months into an eternity.

He had thought of ending his own life – but how would we do it? He thought about hanging, but the concept of choking terrified him. Or an overdose, but what if too small a dose left him paralysed? Or a kitchen knife, but what if he cut the wrong artery? What if souls last an eternity, would the numbness erase instantaneously, or would he be trapped in purgatory until he felt happiness? Or what if he died, and it was just black? The concept of eternal darkness terrified him.

The highs from cocaine happened sporadically. Drugs no longer possessed the euphoria they once encapsulated. Callum now solely took drugs to survive. Without drugs, he was scared what might happen to himself. He thought about how much Taylor consumed his mind. Every thought returned to him; what he could be doing; what he might be thinking about; whether he hated Callum as much as he hated himself. It was an unhealthy obsession he was aware of but the anxious thoughts were more appealing than ever living without him.

It had taken a couple of months for Callum to become obsessed with Taylor and everything about him. Dates, followed by sex, followed by evenings on the sofa together. When Taylor asked Callum if he wanted to stay again, and staying over happened seven nights a week, he knew what it was. When Taylor asked him to become his boyfriend in February, seven months after the first time they met, he was overjoyed. Being homosexual in a working class city that prided itself on masculinity was a struggle, with the prospect of love a mere impossibility. According to Callum, to be with somebody as beautiful as Taylor seemed like an impossibility for any human, not just queer men.

'I could look at you all day,' Callum often said to Taylor. Callum adored every bone in Taylor's body, even when he had hurt him. He often thought about the day that they may get married: his white suit contrasted against Taylor's black; the traditional church; the floral arrangements consisting of roses and hydrangeas; the guests weeping at the exchange of their vows.

He was aware of Taylor's infidelity but allowed it for them to stay together for an eternity. Falling in love and meeting the person you are destined to spend the rest of your life with was everybody's dream in life because society idolised the concept of romantic love. Their relationship was more strained than others, Callum knew, but this was down to his laziness, mood swings, and the disappearance of his libido.

Even after his shower, Callum still felt dirty. The organised mess of their bedroom seemed filthy and suffocating. Dust hung from the ceiling, mould grew across the skirting, and the furniture was archaic. He wanted to decorate the flat more homely, as a favour to Taylor – he knew it would cause a riot if Taylor had zero input in the decoration, which made him bury the thought as imaginative – but never had the monetary expenses or effort to do so.

He checked his phone on the bedroom floor and called his grandmother to no response. He called again. No answer. He called again. No answer.

Hi nan, just checking in on u again. U ok? X Miss you. Call me when you get a chance xx

He counted methodically at the eight unanswered text messages from the past week that had been ignored. He prayed that one day she would forgive him for what he did. He never meant to hurt her; the fact he ever hurt her the way that he had done made his stomach turn.

Just over the road in one of the council houses that had all of the residents in the flats envious – nobody cared to move to a villa in the South of France, or a mansion in Beverly Hills, all they wanted was their own garden with a trampoline – lived a woman nearly double Callum's age he proudly called his only friend. Wendy Johnson was 43 years old and a single mum of two teenage sons: Lucas and Lloyd. 'The father gave them their names; his name is Liam. I chose the girls, he chose the boys,' Wendy had admitted the first time they ever met when Callum had sniggered at the alliteration of the names.

They had met when a parcel was delivered to Wendy by the postman, which led to a 30 minute conversation about the local neighbourhood and how long she had lived on the estate. This small conversation resulted in drinks on the weekend and a friendship ever since. She was maternal, kind, funny, and assertive. She adored her children more than anything and since their father walked out on them five years ago – he had visitation rights whenever, but opted to limit visiting to four times per year – Wendy had become the sole breadwinner of the household.

The youths from the estate could be feral, but Callum thought that Lucas and Lloyd seemed pleasant and well behaved. Wendy had an aged complexion from working late nights and being a single mother, but she was the most positive person that Callum had ever met. At only five-foot three with a stodgy physique, her personality radiated beauty. She nurtured him like a mother, not fond of Taylor and the way he treated Callum. Taylor always told Callum how he thought that Wendy was a villain fuelling his mind with fabrications to manipulate his perception of him. Wendy told him how she believed Taylor was physically and mentally abusive and their relationship only benefitted Taylor. She believed his relationship was lopsided and what Callum wanted, Taylor could never give him.

90% of the time he disagreed with her perception of his relationship. He struggled to find the negative credentials attached to Taylor that Wendy did because he had been brainwashed by an abusive partner.

'Cal. Hello, *love*! How are you?' Wendy answered the door and threw her large arms around him, embracing him like one of her own.

They made their way through the tight entrance of the house, walls filled with so many family photographs hung in frames that you failed to notice the busy floral wallpaper underneath the rows of memories. Callum's favourite was a polaroid of Wendy, Lucas, and Lloyd, hidden in a tiny frame above the boiler cupboard that showed the three of them on Conwy beach. Lucas had a vanilla ice cream cone in his hand whilst Lloyd had his small arms wrapped around Wendy's legs. It was the smile on all three of their faces that made it Callum's favourite.

Entrance into the rectangular kitchen was met with the penetrating smell of acidic detergent that illustrated Wendy was in the middle of cleaning, the floor still wet under his footsteps as he attempted to tread lightly to the dinner table.

'Sit down, love. I'll do you a brew.' She poured the kettle and filled a mug of tea with milk and two sugars: just as he liked. 'Apologies for the smell in here, I've been cleaning.'

'Thanks so much. Have you been okay?'

'Good, Cal. How have you been?'

'I've really not been okay. That's the reason why I visited. I hope you don't mind. You always manage to make me feel better and I really appreciate all the help you do for me.'

'Fire away, son.'

'Okay… this might be a bit of a life story so I apologise if it bores you to death; I will try and keep it short. I lived with my nan since I was three. She is my legal guardian, it went through all of the courts, et cetera. She's amazing, Wend. If you had to draw a picture of a typical wholesome nan, it would be mine. Small, stout, grey hair, smoker, amazing cook,' he smiled tightly.

'Anyway, my mum got pregnant from a one-night stand with my dad when she was about 28. They never saw each other again and then my mum went out for her 30th birthday with friends and met him. He never had any idea that she had me. They ended up together. My nan said my dad was made up to hear that he had another child. He has three others, but I have never met them – I class myself as an only child. So, I cannot remember much from that age, obviously, I was just a baby. Well, I don't ever remember any of the good things, if there was any, but I vividly remember the bad. He used to attack her right in front of me, until blood would be pouring from her head, her lips, everywhere. I remember this, I swear to you, but my nan has also confirmed it. He raped her so many times and I just stood and watched. I went mute after that until I was six. How strange? I do remember; I swear to you. How could I remember things so vividly when I was that young? I know you probably think I'm making this up… but I do.'

'I believe you, babe. Honestly. The brain is so strange.'

'I remember how she used to stare at me with her face pressed against the floor when he was on top of her… lying in a pool of her own tears incapable of moving for what seemed like hours after. My nan said that I would eventually soil myself and be left in a nappy full of poo for hours afterwards. He got her on the gear; the heavy stuff, though. *Heroin.* Music blaring at three in the morning; complaints from the police; random men coming in the house whilst I stood at the stop of the stairs with a full nappy. This was all part of the evidence in court. They would glance at me, go into the living room, and close the door. He had been pimping her out. She had left her job and he was a bum, they needed money to feed their addictions so he decided to sell the mother of his child to disgusting old men. I often wonder how much they would charge for a bit of gear. It was rhythmic. Terrible parenting. Of course, as they usually do, social services never helped, no matter how much the nursery reported it. It died down, then I went in with a black eye and that is when I was put in emergency care. My mum had taken an overdose the night before and was rushed to hospital. She was in a coma for a couple of days. I've not had contact with either of them since. Thank God. I have no idea whether they're dead or alive. I hope she left him and I hope he's dead. My nan put herself through all of the system to get me in her care. A widow, 60 years old and basically adopted me as her own. She loved me unconditionally. Gave every penny from her pocket to make sure that I lived a good life. Speech therapy; private counselling; the latest toys; school trips. Everything. She sacrificed her life as a... she would *hate* me for saying this... fucking *pensioner* to make sure that I grew up as normal as I could. Tutors as well, I forgot. £35 an hour for an English tutor when I was falling behind in my GCSEs. She argued with doctors for years until I was diagnosed with Asperger's, which is basically a form of social autism... if you hadn't noticed already.'

'I hadn't noticed to be honest, Cal. You don't have to explain yourself to me anyway, babe. Nothing wrong with that,' Wendy interjected, brushing her warm hand against his arm.

'Thank you. Where was I? Ummm... oh, yes. My nan, she never let it stop me from achieving anything that I wanted. I defied the grades expected of me in school and went on to sixth form and got good grades again. I worked in a care home whilst I was at uni, you know all that. But I got sacked, and then basically failed my course. I was never going in, or if I did, I was hours late and couldn't do anything right. Why did I do that, though? I loved working in care, it was honestly the best job I think I will ever have. It opened my mind up to so many things: disabilities; the elderly; how to care for people; compassion. Sorry, I am digressing… anyway, my relationship with my nan had deteriorated over the past couple of months. I lived with her until I moved in with Taylor. I've took drugs in the past a couple of times but I never liked it, not really a big drinker, I loved my job, my uni course, my life. Now… I just don't know what is up with me. I don't know who I am sometimes. But I have no effort to change anything – do you understand what I mean?'

'I get what you are saying, Callum. It is most definitely depression, babe. Maybe a touch of anxiety, too. You should go to the doctors and see what they could give you. Your nan sounds lovely, so what has happened? Cal, I know you hate me saying it, but your relationship is not healthy. You deserve so much more. He is an absolute fucker. That is why you are in the position you are in. Not because of yourself – because of him. He is honestly one of the worst people I know. He is the definition of a wanker.' Callum knew this would happen. If he relied on Wendy for maternal support, she would give him the hard truth. Whether he believed it or not was irrelevant.

'Want another brew? Wait on telling me the rest until the kettle is boiled. I won't be able to hear you.'

They made small talk about Wendy and the new laundry detergent that gave Lloyd an allergic reaction, the weather for October being relatively warmer than usual, but the Met expecting it to plummet to freezing levels within the next two weeks, and her shift pattern for the week ahead.

'They said they would put me on days whilst the kids are in school but the bastards have got me on lates, again. Lucky for me the boys are old enough to look after themselves... well I think they are, if I leave them for a few hours of a night. Still going through the CMS for money off that waste of space they call a father.'

'Thanks, Wend. I owe you teabags. So I have seen my nan about five times since I moved out and I promised myself I would never ever get like that. I always said I would go down twice a week, at least. Either for tea on my own, or with Taylor. You would honestly love my nan – she just radiates positivity. She is so kind that it is unbelievable. However, she met Taylor and seemed to hate him from day one. He smoked a joint in her back garden when he asked if he could go outside for a smoke and she assumed it was a cigarette. Kicked up a big fuss, I told her she had the wrong impression of him because he was actually nice. She agreed with me and then invited us around again. They argued about something – I cannot remember the specifics. Something pathetic, but you know when arguments get heated and there is an argument to try and get the last word rather than arguing about anything with substance? Digressing again, sorry.'

'I hate that. Another reason why I try and not drink,' Wendy said.

'I went to see her the other week and I'm not going to lie, I had about an hour's sleep. Me and Tay had been up all night. On it, of course. She started lecturing me about what I was doing with my life, saying I was wasting all my potential to satisfy Taylor, that he was bad for me, and that I was becoming a failure. She was saying she knew he was a cokehead and that I was on drugs. I lied and told her I would never do that, and she said I was going to end up like my mum and dad. Is that true – do you think, Wend? At the time, I thought, how could she say that? The stuff they put me through. Now I can't help thinking that she was telling the truth. I have become an evil human being… but I just don't have the effort to try and change myself. I'm so lazy and numb to everything. Anyway, it got heated. I was so tired that I was getting more aggressive just because I needed sleep. I shouted at her, telling her to shut up, and she never. She was getting so upset. Her voice was shaking when she was shouting at me; trying to drill her opinions in my head. I never listened. I was ready to explode. And I did. She was calling him a disgusting rat who would amount to nothing and I just remember shouting at her and then I… I slapped her across the face, Wendy. My actual nan. I hit my own nan. My own mother, basically,' Callum had gone from emotionless to floods of tears. He stood up and paced around the kitchen methodically whilst Wendy sat processing the information that had been relayed to her. She could only see Callum as a polite, timid, young lad – so she struggled to imagine the capability of him being so truculent.

'Cal, to be honest with you... I'm lost for words. We all make mistakes, first and foremost. You are not a bad person, honestly. I think you need to go and see your nan, knock at her door, and sincerely apologise to her... I'm sorry but you need help with your mental health and to get rid of that relationship. Seriously, how often are you taking drugs?'

'Only about once a week,' Callum lied.

'Don't lie to me, love. You can be honest with me, you know that.'

'Okay... maybe... five or six times a week.'

'God, Cal. Once a week is enough as it is. Six times a week is *shocking*. You need to stop that. The damage that must be doing to your body. That is an addiction, love. No wonder you feel terrible; you seriously need to get out of that relationship, Callum. You deserve so much better – do you think that you would be doing drugs like that if you were single or with somebody else?'

'Ummm... maybe. I don't like to think of what ifs,' Callum said.

'I don't think you would be in the position you are in if you never met him. You have to agree with that? He is a narcissist and a manipulator.'

'No, no, no. You just see the downs that we have. Honestly, we are good together. Just sometimes he can be a tad bit moody. But so can I. Don't we all have mood swings? Honestly, he is a nice person, I promise you,' Callum said, struggling to believe the words coming out of his own mouth.

'Oh, Cal. You are only kidding yourself. He is not a nice person to you, but if you are happy, then who am I to judge? We all see good in people that we love more than others do. My honest advice is to use your brain and not just your heart. You are the nicest kid ever; you could get anybody that you wanted. You are so intelligent, handsome, and funny. You have the world ahead of you. Don't snort shit to try and cure whatever you feel inside because it will *never* cure you. It will only make you worse. The more you take, the worse you get. Trust me. I cannot remember if I ever told you this… I used to be a support worker for people suffering with substance abuse; you know in the St Magdalene's Community Centre down the road? I honestly could tell you stories of how many broken people come in and because they didn't want to help themselves, they never. Death; suicide; all that. It's not good, Cal. I'm no saint, I have the odd line now and again, but I know where to draw the line. And even when I do it, I think to myself, why the fuck have I just done that? There is so many beautiful reasons to be happy and that feeling of depression after a session of alcohol and drugs is not one of them.'

Callum loved the bond he shared with Wendy. Although he disagreed with her stance on topics relating to Taylor, he knew that her viewpoint was critical. After all, Wendy was an outsider looking in. He knew she would never be deceitful for no reason because she cared for him – like a long lost mother that he never had.

It took a while of daydreaming before the conversation continued. Callum noticed the new faux plant that stood in the corner of Wendy's kitchen. Dark green, seven-foot tall, wide, inviting.

'I give the kids all I can but when I'm on them comedowns… *wow*. I'm the worst person in the world. It alters your reality and everything you work hard for. Your mental health dwindles. So, you take drugs again thinking that will solve it, but it won't. It's a vicious cycle. The kids' dad is a cokehead… used to go on binges and forget about them. Their birthdays, how old they are, everything. It is heartbreaking watching somebody fall apart right before your eyes. Especially for the boys, they have no clue obviously,' Wendy had got teary-eyed reciting her secrets to Callum. The roles reversed and he was now stroking Wendy's arm, attempting to comfort her.

'Oh, Wendy. I never knew that about Liam. I'm so sorry coming over here and talking about myself when you have your own stuff going on at home.'

'I'm sorry for going on,' Wendy said.

'No, keep going.'

'I loved him. The kids' dad. I still do. The shit he has put me and the kids through shows he doesn't love us, though. My priority in life is my two boys and I am not letting anyone get in between that. I rarely drink, last week I had a few glasses of prosecco and then went to bed. I couldn't do it. I needed to sort stuff out for the boys and tidy around the next day and I knew if I carried on drinking, nothing would get done. That is why you and I are different because you continue to drink and take drugs thinking that something amazing will happen to you or that it will numb the pain or hangover. You stay in a cycle of vicious depression. That's why you need to make amends with your nan. She deserves an apology to her face after what you have done. You have been emotional today; I know you have them feelings. Let them out. Vulnerability is the biggest strength a man can possess.'

'I'm scared in case she wants nothing to do with me ever again,' Callum said.

'I doubt she would do that; she loves you. Hey, if everything goes wrong, at least you can say that you tried.'

They spoke about lighter topics for a while afterwards to ease the mood and Callum's increasing anxiety. Wendy had planned to clean the back garden before the grass frosted over; Callum agreed to assist with nil gardening skills.

Callum felt the burden of stress had slightly lifted once he concluded his visit to Wendy's, spending over an hour and a half in her small kitchen: talking, crying, laughing. His discussion with Wendy about his grandmother had prompted him to take the power into his own hands. He decided to take the usual route which consisted of a bus from their local stop to the city centre, followed by a further bus to the south, concluded with a 25 minute walk on top.

Hi. How u getting on in work today? You tired? X

Taylor usually replied within seconds – out of tedium – so when he failed to text back by the time the first bus had arrived in the city centre, Callum had begun to conjure up the most terrifying scenarios. Death, a freak accident in work and the forklift had annihilated his existence, heavy crates had fell from ten feet high onto his head and broken his neck, or Taylor had enough and tonight would be the night that he would finally leave. Thoughts ran wild through his mind and the building anxiety grew in his chest as he edged closer to confronting the woman he had deeply hurt.

Callum travelled through the suburban area where his grandmother's house was nestled, passing teenagers in their school uniforms, runners, and construction sites of new build houses. Heavy winds blew the crisp autumn leaves across the concrete walkways into the gardens of lawyers' and doctors' houses. The valuation of the houses around the area tripled compared to the vicinity of the flat he resided in. Vast amounts of green hedges covered garden walls with flowerbeds planted throughout the public paths. The south of Liverpool seemed like an alien planet of wealth and glory to Callum now, not somewhere he had grown up and roamed for the entirety of his adolescent life.

The bus was flooded with the elderly rolling shopping trolleys packed with newspapers and potatoes for a Sunday roast dinner, none using mobile phones or technology, soaking up the scenery from the bus window – scenery they had likely passed for 80 years of their lives. Callum often wondered to himself how pensioners enjoyed their life no matter what tribulations were faced. They never turned to social media for instant gratification or an escape from reality, which seemed like an easier way of living.

He wished to be born in a different generation without the societal pressures of eating healthy, being successful in your workplace, and making your peers envious of your trips abroad.

The End is Near

His stomach knotted with anxiety as the bus stopped down a narrow road, indicative of continuing the rest on foot for one and a half kilometres. He pulled a Marlboro cigarette from the box – he preferred Lambert & Butler but the shop had none – and inhaled a long drag, the blissful feeling of nicotine intoxication rushing through his body. Smoking was not a habit Callum aimed to take up in his younger years but his reliance on tobacco was something that he did not want to give up the more that he smoked, especially when his mental health was ruined. It calmed him.

Callum noticed and felt every view and sensation that he walked past. How the trees arched and the leaves submitted to the seasonal changes, tones of butter and burnt orange: the quintessential autumnal palette. The grey slabs of concrete seemed darker as the weather was colder, and when the icy wind blew it sent a shiver through Callum's body.

Callum lit another cigarette with the flame of his first and threw the butt on the floor. He checked his mobile phone once more and noticed that Taylor had responded.

Fine

Fine? He started to analyse every aspect of the four-letter word and all of its potential meanings. The short response from Taylor was another stressor added to his ever-growing anxiety, less than five minutes away from his childhood home. He must have done something wrong, Callum thought, because whenever Taylor text him that he was fine, it usually meant the opposite. The nicotine had resulted in increased blood pressure and shallow breathing that bordered on panic.

He turned left and headed down the cul-de-sac, home to where his grandmother Agnes had lived for over fifty years. The two-storey home that was buried in the right corner looked the same as when he had left it. The original brick was untouched with a bright red front door nestled to the right, next to the adjacent neighbour. He wondered how a woman of 79 years of age could still manage to move up and down the stairs multiple times a day and why she had never asked the council for a bungalow.

'When you ask for a bungalow, love, that's when you know you are close to death. The minute I cannot get up these stairs is the minute that I want you to put a needle in me and end my pain,' he had remembered her saying. He sniggered at the remembrance of her sharp but witty tongue.

As Callum descended down the road and through her front path, he had noticed that the lilies planted in the front garden had begun to dwindle to the heavy rainfall they had experienced recently and the lilac painted bench underneath the rectangular window was beginning to chip, the copper fittings rusty. Petals from no-longer-with-us flowers declined from the hanging baskets pillared at the front door in a direction that made them shrug away every visitor. It was definite that her home was for the summer seasons and the decrease in temperature gave it the illusion of being uninviting, like an old witch's lair.

Callum ripped away the deadheads on the outskirts of one of the hanging baskets when the heavy door opened, revealing Agnes, a stone expression spread across her face. He wondered in his head whether his behaviour was a prime factor in her diminishing beauty and drastic weight loss. She had always looked after herself with cheap creams and minimal time in the sun, but Agnes had never looked worse, even if old age was a key reason for her loss of collagen. Agnes' wrinkles had quadrupled and she was the thinnest she had ever been.

'Hello, nan. It's nice to see you,' Callum said gingerly.

'What are you doing to my baskets? Leave them bloody alone. Have you come here to ruin something else? Get away from my house, Callum.'

Callum continued to take in his grandmother's appearance as she stood at the door. She was tiny, four-foot eleven with a face that told stories of years of work, heartbreak, and loss. Her thin grey hair was strung loose on her head and she wore a gingham apron over her clothes, her usual fluffy slippers on. Her name had Grecian roots, meaning "pure" and "holy" – just as Callum saw her. The stern expression retracted his willingness to be open the way imagined. Would this be another bout of rejection that he could not cope with? he thought to himself. Rejection played a crucial part in Callum's underlying lack of esteem and to be rejected by his guardian angel was not something he thought he would be able to endure. Fear that this could be the thing that ended him once and for all. It was peculiar how one's own mistakes could lead those who promised you a lifetime to give up on you. How your lack of initiative in an instance could diminish decades worth of trust with every memory disintegrated to a past life.

He realised that he needed to bury his ego and be as fragile as possible. This frail, tired woman had dedicated so much of her life to him and he owed her the world and every star that orbited it.

'Callum, is there a reason why you have turned up unannounced at my door?'

'Sorry, I was just getting rid of the dead flowers in the basket… the weather has gone horrible and they looked a little droopy,' Callum replied, still plucking at the dead flowers in the basket. They awkwardly stood in silence for a while.

'Callum? What the fuck are you still doing here, love?' Agnes continued; dismissing him with her frail loose-skinned hands.

'I was just popping down to see if you were okay.'

'I am. Is that all?'

'Nan, please. Can I just come in for a second? I need to talk to you and apologise for what I did.' The door left ajar; Callum accompanied her back inside. He followed her through the tiny hall, floral red and blue wallpaper and mahogany flooring covering the room's entirety. The living room at Agnes' home was rarely used and any social soirées with Phyllis and Vera visiting with a bottle of brandy was limited to the small white wooden table in the kitchen that sat four, upholstered with floral pattern seats in purple and green.

The kitchen was flooded with an unnecessary number of oak cupboards that were bare inside and dirty white tiles on the floor, mopped bimonthly. Although slightly dusty, the room was alluring and cosy and Agnes always had a fresh bouquet of the cheapest flowers from the local florist in the middle of the dining table.

'Do you need me to do any cleaning or anything whilst I am here, nan?'

'Oh, love. I am perfectly capable of doing that myself, as you can see. There is not a thing out of place in here.'

Callum noted Agnes' comments and surveyed the room where he could see fragments of mud and crumbs dotted around the kitchen floor, cigarette ash on the kitchen table, dirty glasses in the sink, and yellow stains on the walls, but chose not to mention anything to avoid the probability of further conflict.

He made himself a cup of tea and Agnes coffee – her usual yellow mug stained brown from overuse – in complete silence. The nicotine stained blinds in the kitchen were wide open which revealed that the weather had further deteriorated, now heavily raining: typical British autumnal weather. Callum dreaded the journey home.

'S-so nan… I think it is time that we finally have a talk about what happened.'

She sniggered before starting. 'A talk? There is nothing to talk about, love. You hit your grandmother, not even your grandparent actually, your wee fucking parent in the eyes of the law and I will never talk to you ever again for what you did to me.'

'Okay… I never meant a talk… I meant that I need to apologise. I am deeply sorry for what I did to you. For being so nasty with my words, for hitting you, for shouting at you, for not being the best grandson to you, for everything. For even being alive.' She sniggered again; this time more exaggerated.

'Do not dare try and manipulate me to feel sorry for you by saying things like "sorry for being alive" because it is not going to work on me.

I would never wish bad on you because it is not who I am.' Agnes lit a cigarette and inhaled a long drag before she continued.

'I told you that I never want to see your face ever again. What you did to me, what you said to me... I will never ever forgive you. I love you with all of my heart but what you did to me was unforgiveable. Who have you become as a person? You are not my lad; I definitely know that. Not the Callum that I know. I have no idea who you are now. Whatever that relationship of yours is has turned you into a monster. I blame that bastard you are with.'

'Nan, honestly. It is nothing to do with Taylor for what I did the other day... I am so sorry for behaving like that. It was despicable and out of character. I should never have laid my hands on you. I swear I never meant it. I have had a lot of things going on that I just can't explain. I'm sorry for what I did.'

'You are defending him already. You can't see any side of the story besides your own when it involves something to do with him. You are so far up his backside that it is untrue.'

'Oh, nan. Please don't be like that. You have met him at the wrong time, honestly. He is really nice, I promise. He really likes you too,' Callum lied. Taylor hated Agnes and Callum was aware of that fact. He said that she was arrogant, evil, and could get away with being grotesque because she was a pensioner.

'Ha. I don't give a toss what that idiot thinks of me. Even if he wanted me fucking dead I would not give a flying fuck. He's a drug addict.'

'*No*, he's not. Honestly, he's nothing like that. He's a nice boy. He does well for himself... he isn't to blame for what I did to you, that was all me. I'm so sorry again.'

'Does well for himself? Living in a bedsit with you as his slave... I'm sure he does. That boy is a druggie, don't you lie to me,' Agnes said viciously, shooing Callum away with her frail hands. 'He is a narcissistic bastard and the sooner you walk away from him, the better. Until then, I do not want anything to do with you. You are not my Callum anymore – you are a monster. You are your mother and your father combined.'

Her final sentence made Callum's stomach turn. He had become his parents and he knew it. An addict. Selfish. Controlled by his partner. Evil. No wonder she hated him, he had become the epitome of everything that his grandmother despised.

Callum vaguely remembered a memory from when he was around eight years old, when he snuck into Agnes' bedroom, and found her sat on the edge of bed weeping for no apparent reason. He remembered that he had hit Paul Sampson during playtime in school because he called him stupid. She had to leave work early to pick him up which meant a pay deduction for herself and the dependant she cared for. He fought back tears as his nan continued to talk, unable to listen to a word that she had said whilst reminiscing on a distant memory. Callum had concluded that she was never going to forgive him; he was fighting a losing battle with no hope of reconciliation.

'Nan... please... I never came here to argue with you. I sincerely apologise again for what I have done. I am so sorry for what I did and said the other day. I had hardly slept that night and I had a lot of things going on in my head that made me react like that.'

'I wonder why that was. You were on all kinds of drugs all night, as usual! Did you actually not learn nothing from your own mum and dad? Did that not scare you enough?' She had become more angry the more she spoke, the muscles in her neck tightening through every word. 'Callum, I never brought you up to be wasting money on disgusting habits like smoking cannabis and sniffing cocaine.'

'*I don't*, I promise. The things I said to you were disgusting. But I hope you can try to forgive me. I promise that I will try and make it up to you. You have done so much for me and I repay you like that.'

'Too right, it is bloody disgusting. You are a disgrace to my name. What you did was unforgiveable and I do not want to see you again,

Callum.' Agnes wept into her hands as Callum departed the house, which would be the last time he ever saw her.

'I love you,' he muttered as he left the room. And there it was. The one person he thought would never, had given up on him. If his own grandmother could turn on him, didn't that mean Taylor could? The inherited DNA integrated through their bodies was not enough to make her hold on. He thought he may have cried more than the few tears he did, but the paralysis succumbed all other emotions. When the numbness sank in – the immobility to care also plagued over him. Is this what he would feel when he potentially got a new job he should be excited to start? Or when he hopefully got married in the future? Or a mortgage on a house? What a sad world to live in when the second greatest bereavement in his life could not release any emotion from within. He made his way towards the bus stop and home to the only person he felt somewhat safe with.

CHAPTER THREE

On the same day of Callum's heartbreaking discovery that Agnes had decided to abandon him, Taylor's day at the wholesalers finished just after seven o'clock in the evening, an hour after closing to the public which meant further cleaning, counting inventory, sorting pre-orders for pick up, and moving stock. The drug-stocked night prior – he remembered an argument that him and Callum had over the TV remote that resulted in Callum slapping him across the face – made his day at work one of the most gruelling, even though he was regularly hungover in work. He had fallen asleep for twenty minutes during his dinner break and had retched endlessly throughout the day.

For a peculiar reason he had no understanding of, he strangely missed Callum when he arose from his accidental nap, and longed to get home for the entirety of their evening to be spent together. It was very rare that he missed Callum – he usually loathed his existence and being in proximity – so when he did; he felt sex mandatory.

He had planned for them to order a takeaway – unsure where to get the funds from, he owed hundreds out in money for drug debts and his overdraft was nearly maxed out – to watch a thriller on the sofa – thriller was his favourite genre, Callum opted for rom-com or horror – whilst they had sex and remained sober for a night.

As Taylor entered his keys into the front door of the flat, he noted the sound of melancholic music pulsating through the walls at an intense volume. He was unsure who the artist was. Maybe Lana Del Rey, Adele, or Fiona Apple. He never shared an interest in the music that Callum listened to, even when Callum pretended to like Queen or The Rolling Stones in order to please his dominant master. The last thing that Taylor needed after a long day in work on minimal sleep was to hear depression on full volume throughout the flat.

He kicked his shoes off in the hall and saw Callum drunkenly singing to an empty beer bottle in the living room: disassociated from his surroundings, swaying nonchalantly from side to side with his eyes closed, and stumbling on every incorrect lyric.

Discarded bottles of beer lay on the sofa with a haze fogging the room from excessive smoking. An ashtray full of Callum's cigarette butts sat on the arm of the sofa; Taylor knew this as fact because the ashtray had been emptied the night prior. Taylor watched his monthly salary being wasted right before his eyes which sent a streak of anger through his body.

'Callum!' Taylor shouted repeatedly to no response; Callum so drunk that he never noticed his boyfriend enter until the music had stopped.

'What the fu-... oh, hi, Tay! I have *missed* you today,' Callum stumbled and fell into Taylor's grip, tripping on an empty beer bottle that had leaked on the carpet, a large stain growing underneath his foot.

'Callum, what the fuck are you doing? You know what downstairs are like and you have got *that shit* on loud. Are you joking? You couldn't even hear me come in through the door. You know we could have the council around *again*.' Taylor was raged at the thought of another visit from the council, who had received reports of antisocial behaviour and high noise levels on several occasions to the point they risked eviction. 'I can't even trust you to be left alone for a couple of hours whilst I go and work like a normal adult.'

'Oh, is that right? I'm the worst person in the world because I have the music on. How silly. Are you not even going to... to... ask me if I'm okay?'

A night of intimacy now seemed to be off the cards and Taylor realised that the evening could end in battle between the pair.

'Do not *ever* talk to me like that again. What the fuck are you doing, Callum?' he said, 'I'm sorry, I never meant to shout at you.'

'I've had a *reallyyy* fucking bad day today. A *reallyyy* bad day. And you come in here and start hitting me for *no* fucking reason,' Callum slurred.

'I never hit you, I grabbed your arm. I tried to calm you down. I said sorry. What has happened today?'

'No, don't pretend like you care about what I have to say. You hit me for no fucking reason.'

'Okay, whatever. Don't tell me then.' It took a while for Callum to explain the situation between talking with Wendy and visiting Agnes. Taylor chose not to visit Agnes on that day. He hated Agnes, but sympathised with Callum on family members giving up on you. Taylor had a strained relationship with both of his parents because of his explosive father. However, the relationship had been strained since his early teens because of who Taylor chose to socialise with, his habits, and his ever increasing debt, partially funded by their bank accounts.

'Oh God, Cal. I feel awful. Not sure what else to say, to be honest. You don't need her; I know that for a fact.'

'That's it? That's all you have to say. You are one *selfish* bastard.' Callum cried. 'You do not give a fuck about me. You do not give a fuck about anyone but yourself. Your boyfriend has had a bad day and all you can say is, "I feel awful." So you should as well, you have caused all of this.'

Callum walked over to the Bluetooth speaker and turned the volume up loud. Taylor interjected by pulling the plug from its socket and launching the speaker across the living room – leaving it unrepairable, shattered to the floor with a heavy thud. Carole King's concert ceased immediately.

'What the fuck are you doing? You have broken that and we both listen to it.'

'Lose your *fucking* attitude with me, Callum. I'm serious. I have caused all of this? Who said that? That fat tramp up the road, Wendy? We all have bad days… some of us actually have bad days at work if we bothered to leave the fucking house and get a job.'

'Wow… you are one nasty person, Taylor. Leave me alone. I actually hate you.' Callum continued to slur his words, sitting on the edge of the sofa nonchalantly.

'How am I a nasty person, Cal? I've been in work all day… I have not said a single word to you except to turn that off because the neighbours complain. They have probably already complained if you have had that on for hours. All I wanted tonight was to come home and have a fucking peaceful night with you watching a film or something. But you decide to blast music and swirl around the living room like a fucking fairy spending all of my hard-earned money on ale. It's out of order.'

'Taylor, you are the biggest narcissist ever! All you care about is yourself. We are in a relationship, have been for over eight months, and you can't even ask me how my fucking day has been. I'm drinking because I feel down.'

'Callum, don't try and turn this all round on me for actually wanting to go to work! I'm working to keep us in this fucking flat, unlike what you are doing. You are so entitled you little prick… I'm trying to keep this roof over our heads and it's Christmas in a couple of months. Go and get a fucking job. You are starting to piss me off, to be honest with you.'

'I can't believe you've just said that. You know I want to go back to work so much. I tell you every single day that I do!'

'Yeah, Callum, you tell me you want to work, that's it. You don't get out of bed and go and find a job, you just dwell on your past constantly. You are the laziest person I know. You weren't like this when I first met you. All of them plans we had. We haven't done one fucking thing together,' Taylor said matter-of-factly. 'Going to work every morning and seeing you still asleep in bed knowing you are still going to be there for hours after pisses me off so much. Maybe we need to stop drinking so often.'

'Taylor. A few drinks now and again is nothing to worry about,' Callum lied, intoxicated, vowing every day that he would never drink again.

'It starts with a few and then we are up for days, dreading the rest of the week, until it all repeats again. I feel like death today. I had a nap on my dinner in the staffroom. I never nap… never mind in work.'

'I hate the way we do this. One minute we are so good together then we fight. It's constant. I feel like I'm walking on eggshells with you all of the time. Thinking you will snap for the smallest inconvenience. I don't think you understand how low I feel and how much I hate myself and you never ask me how I'm feeling but it's probably because you don't even care about me! You just think I'm lazy. Taylor, I'm really not in a good space. I'm scared,' Callum said.

'Of course I care. I know I can be hot-headed sometimes but I don't mean it, Cal. Sorry.' As he apologised, Taylor took a step forward and put his arms around Callum in an attempt to defuse the situation. Callum snatched himself from his grip and froze still. No physical touch or false sense of caring.

'No, Taylor, just listen to what I have to say. For once, please. This feeling I have inside of me is really not okay. I hate feeling like this, but I'm dealing with so much inside that I do not feel *anyyything* at all. I have this constant dread of waking up and thinking wow, another day doing this, seriously? I'd rather be dead sometimes.'

'Callum, you don't mean that. You're drunk.'

'She's had enough of me, Taylor. She actually hates me. My own nan, who gave me everything, protected me from everything bad in the world... hates me. I went to see her today and she said that she would never forgive me for what I did to her. She said that I'm a monster. Taylor, for her to say that I must have really hurt her because that woman has been through a lot in her life. I have disappointed her legacy and myself.'

He wondered how many other people across the eight billion living on Earth would be dealing with heartache like he was. He knew he would not be alone, but he felt it. Callum felt like nobody on the planet would understand the depression eating him alive.

'You are *not* a monster, Cal. I promise you. Don't listen to what she says. She has no idea who you are as a person anymore because she makes no effort to even visit you. That's why she said that – guilt. Come on, lad. You can't keep being like this... you just need to get over it.'

The End is Near

'Get over it? That's all you have to say. You are honestly pathetic at times; you do know that? Let me just switch my fucking brain off and get over it with a click of my fingers.'

Large drops of rain smashed the windows violently, the wind howling through the branches of the English oak tree in the front of their shared lawn. The halt from aerobic movement – in the form of dancing to ballads – around the flat had made Callum realise that the temperature had drastically declined, the central heating in the flat unable to warm up the premises. Callum worried further communication would cause another argument so he sat in silence; cigarette in hand.

Callum had decided that communicating with Taylor would be fighting a losing battle. Taylor never cared about his opinion, or his feelings, or how his actions hurt him. Purging himself from the situation was the correct solution to defuse the state of affairs. He trotted off to their bedroom. Red and cream floral wallpaper on a single wall behind the bed, cheap brown carpet on the floor, and nothing much else except an oak double bed, cheap wooden furniture, and a small TV in the left corner. It sometimes felt like a budget hotel room.

'Where the fuck do you think you are going? Shouting your mouth off at me then just taking yourself to bed.' Taylor placed a gentle hand on

Callum's elbow, 'I'm sorry, Callum. Please just ignore me,' but Callum shunned it away forcefully. As an act of retaliation, Taylor had pushed Callum with such force that he fell to the floor with a heavy thud. Taylor thought about the first time he met Callum when he worked as a care worker. A care worker who intended to run his own agency in the future. A boy once full of aspiration. This aspiration soon diminished after they continued their sexual affair and Taylor realised how easy Callum could be manipulated. The strong mind he thought he possessed was an illusion.

It felt normal and thrilling to be pushed as the warm feeling of blood rushed to his face. Blood had begun to erupt from Callum's nose as his face shattered at the hands of his lover. Taylor punched him in the stomach several times, pinned him to the floor, and unbuttoned his jeans.

Callum knew what was to come.

It was not the first time and would never be the last.

His future imitated childhood trauma: he was his mother. A whore unworthy of love. When Callum was blank of expression, Taylor aggressively pulled Callum's underwear off to reveal his white legs and intimate areas, exposed and meritless. He wondered what thrill Taylor got from non-consensual sex with his partner. Was it a sense of dominance that men could thrive off? Ridicule? Disgust? Desperation? He never knew, but Callum knew how it made himself feel.

'Please, Taylor. I don't want to do this tonight. Please,' Callum said quietly.

'I don't care what you feel like. You are doing this whether you like it not. That's what good boyfriends do,' he stepped out of his jeans that he had worn for work, revealing his underwear bulging with an erection. It made Callum's stomach turn that a lack of consent could arouse his partner so much. Taylor continued to ignore his boyfriend's pleas as he forced himself inside. The tears rolled from his eyes and fell to the carpet underneath his skin.

'Make yourself look like you're enjoying this.' Callum knew to do as he was told to make the torture end quicker. With an accumulation of negative thoughts at the forefront of his brain; he managed a faint smile, enough to satisfy Taylor. Taylor plunged in and out at momentum. He placed his thick hands around Callum's throat until he finally ejaculated; releasing a loud cry throughout the flat. Callum did not take his eyes off the ceiling as he lay dormant. Dormant at the realisation that his boyfriend had just sexually assaulted him, again.

'Let's get into bed,' Taylor casually said after sexually abusing his partner.

As Callum lay processing what had just occurred, the concept of love came to his thoughts. Love seemed to be an ideology constructed by society to make people think fulfilment was in the hands of somebody else. For companies to profit off all the books and movies that generated them billions a year, then the heartbreak that came with it also generated billions a year in the form of ballads and more books and movies. He thought how sad it was that the fetishization of love and heartbreak made society operate efficiently.

'Fuck. You look like a corpse, Callum,' Taylor joked, but Callum could not bring himself to laugh, or talk, or move; paralysed from disgust. Following a few painful minutes of silence, Taylor had departed the bedroom to cook food in the tiny square kitchen and Callum found the departure to be bliss.

How could one of the worst offences known to mankind be acceptable behind closed doors with your partner? Was Callum only destined for a relationship comprised of non-consensual sex? He wanted passion, love-making, neck kisses, deep conversations. He closed his eyes to invoke tears but nothing came. He felt nothing because he now realised that he knew no better. Prone to evilness since infancy with no evidence of the evil slowing. No other emotions could surface so he decided to sleep; instantly falling asleep for the first time in forever.

The End is Near

Callum woke from a deep sleep in the middle of the night, a pool of sweat covering his pillow and upper body, a soaring temperature and violent back pain from their uncomfortable mattress. He panted for breath and it took a while to take in the usual surroundings and readjust back to normalcy. He had had another one of his night terrors and this one the most vivid in a long time.

Callum was sat on a cold, metal chair in the middle of an empty dark room. Taylor, Agnes, and both of his parents sat around him with dim overhead lighting above them, like a crime drama with a criminal held for ransom in a derelict building. The four of them were all deformed into the worst possible versions of themselves he could imagine. Agnes with three arms that morphed into tentacles and her usual small physique was now grotesquely large, webbed feet bursting from her slippers. She had repeatedly chanted how much she hated him and wished he was killed by his father. His parents were the worst substance abuse victims ever encountered, blisters and bruises covering the entirety of their bodies. They both injected heroin in front of him, no matter how much he pleaded resistance. The worst part of his terror was that Taylor was not sat alone; he was entertained by six men hanging from all over his body who looked near identical to himself; whispering things into Taylor's ear as he sat naked in the middle of the room being taunted by the eyes on him. He was unable to move and unable to wake himself up. When he finally woke and saw black, he felt petrified.

His mind raced back to the night before and Taylor fucking him hard on the bedroom floor without his consent. He felt uneasy inside for a second but retracted his thought process because now that he was sober he realised that he was in the wrong, not Taylor. Unknowingly manipulated, Callum believed that Taylor had physiological needs and did what needed to be done for pleasure. He struggled being submissive which resulted in feuds, Taylor assaulting him, and regret the next day.

It was just after two a.m. when Callum proceeded to the bathroom and rinsed his face with cold water, the chill resuscitating him back to his familiar surroundings of the grimy bathroom. With the uncertainty of his night terror; he felt more vulnerable than ever. Approaching the bed slowly like a sleeper agent, he spread the used towel out as far as possible along his allotted side: the reminders of the night terror wet on his skin. His pillow was soaking with perspiration from his thick hair as he wiped it in a pathetic attempt to salvage it.

'Taylor. Taylor. Wake up. I had a bad dream.' Taylor had always slept naked – something that had been an occurrence since the first time they met – because he said it made him feel claustrophobic to sleep in underwear. Callum inhaled deeply at the musty smell of his naked chest that was covered with thick dark hair.

'Huh?' he grumbled.

'Sorry to wake you. I had a bad dream.'

'I'm sorry to hear that,' Taylor said gently. He placed a kiss on Callum's head and they cuddled in silence for a while. Although they only had sex a couple of hours prior, when Taylor entered his cock inside of his hole for the second time that evening, Callum felt as tight as a virgin.

'Sorry, that was quick. I was half asleep,' Taylor muttered. Callum felt instant gratification that he had just made his lover come so fast, and breathed a sigh of relief that maybe there could be a happy ending to their relationship.

'I love you,' Callum said.

'You too. I'm sorry about before.'

'It was all my fault.'

'I suppose so,' Taylor said.

There was no further conversation between the pair. It did not take long for the familiar feeling of loneliness to sink in.

The End is Near

CHAPTER FOUR

The months approached the end of the year with only six days until Christmas. The colourless streets where Taylor and Callum resided had widespread issues of poverty and depression, hidden within the cracks of cold tacky homes decorated with crushed velvet and diamante furnishings.

Signs of Christmas nowhere to be found except for crooked lights hung from trees – cheaply decorated by the council with the measly remains of their slashed budgets – only to be torn down and set on fire by local thugs, additional cheap tinsel lining the local pubs and stores in an attempt to roll the punters in and leave them with even less spending power over Christmas. A vicious cycle prevailed how those crippled by the economic austerity of the country – caused by an incompetent government – felt that the only way they could survive the festive period was to make every effort to drain their own class of people to line their own pockets.

Trepidation settled in further as the big day got closer, loose change wedged down the arm of the sofa now slumped together to get as close to something of value as possible. Fathers worked multiple jobs whilst mothers stayed at home tending to their children; aiding the home's soul as the other half tended to the foundations. Sleepless nights from being stressed, overworked, and underpaid. Stress of whether their children would be waking up with happy faces for one short morning of the year, whilst they scraped at the lining of their purses and wallets for money for the bills; foodbank tokens becoming normality for the following weeks after luxury living over the festive period. The cold weather, lack of expenses, and forced festive outings led to more deaths from pneumonia, more stabbings from drug-fuelled idiots in local pubs, more pressure on the government to fix the corrupt system, and more successful suicide attempts.

Andy Williams sung of how *It's the Most Wonderful Time of the Year*, but to who? Christmas was the most wonderful time of the year to the elite who were unshackled from the housing system, or people who had all of their family members alive and surrounding them at the dinner table, but not to these folk. Sadness ran through the core of Liverpool at this time of year. A time of stress; grief; abandonment; deprivation. The local newspapers were stuffed with black and white bleeding print of passages to the other side; arrests for attempted murders and drink driving fatalities; local politicians found dead at their homes; another low-paid sector on strike criticised by the faulty and abhorrent government for their disruptions. It was also a time for façade to pretend that everything was going smoothly.

Callum had found a job working in a local fish and chip shop, Mike's, a month prior to Christmas – the stench of grease, sweat, and minimum wage his new cologne – and his part-time hours had upped from 20 to a gruelling average of 60, worked to the bone for a mere £9.50 an hour with hundreds of pounds robbed by the taxman every month. He often wondered where all of his tax money was going to – the lack of new infrastructure and jobs was something that ought to be queried. He had the strongest suspicion that the money was being funnelled into the pockets of the elite to make them richer and those struggling even poorer, but this concept would always be a mystery to common folk.

Council tax was forever increasing, yet he noted no changes to his environment: binmen not doing their job resulted in heaps of bags of waste stacked high down alleyways; deep potholes misaligned in the roads making it unsteady for vehicles to drive; streets dark and eery with no lights failing to illuminate the dead of the night. Binbags rose high behind Mike's because the binmen had been on strike for two weeks – citing better pay as the key ask – which was another sign of his economic contributions to society failing to be shown. The alleyways were apparently sorted every week but it had been a long time since he went out the back and noticed anything less than a battlefield of black polyethylene.

Energy bills were capped at the highest rate on record, families all over the country deciding whether to heat their homes or feed their children. Foodbanks were begging for charitable donations for any ultra-processed food they could get as those in need were multiplying into larger numbers daily.

Rent regulation laws flew out the window, council house tenants getting more expensive direct debits taking out every month – metaphorical for society evaporating into a huge pile of shit.

As much as Callum tried to get festive, he struggled to find the joy that the advertisements depicted. He could not think of one piece of art that accurately depicted the struggles of December in a working class environment. The soap operas that intended to reflect the society of its viewers were doing a poor job. Producers' assumptions that happiness at Christmas being a catalyst for viewer ratings was a shortcoming – the concept of painting over all of the flaws of actuality offensive to viewers because society now longed for a sense of reality.

60 hours a week meant plenty more money. More money = more spent on Taylor = a happier Taylor = a happier him. But what he failed to add in this simple mathematical equation was: longer hours = more exhausted = less leisure time to shop = heightened anxiety that he was running out of time before the 25th came around = falling back into their old habits of arguing over trivia.

The End is Near

With every second of downtime that he got at work Callum surfed the internet – Amazon; JD Sports; Sports Direct; Argos; Next; Hugo Boss; Instagram; Facebook; back to Amazon; back to Sports Direct. He bought useless gifts to fill the anxiety, four packs of Nike socks to be delivered from Amazon when there was no storage space for another pair, a new engraved lighter with a marijuana plant and his name on the front, and a voucher for a day on a steam-engine train round Yorkshire in May for the pair of them. He questioned his integrity after every pathetic purchase.

He needed to see clothes in person to buy them – to feel materials because he knew how picky Taylor could be about polyester blends rubbing against his skin, and to decide which size would fit him best – but never had the time or energy to face the city centre without the risk of a panic attack.

On the 19th day of December, it was 5:30 p.m. and he had another five hours left of monotony before he could go home and see Taylor. He effortlessly folded paper lined with fish, chips, sausages, and chop suey, and placed the food into thin plastic bags as customers came in and out the door rapidly. He robotically addressed all with the same polite feminine voice. Orders for kitchen staff were written in shorthand that layperson would find illegible like ancient Sanskrit. The only good thing about working extra hours was how fast time went because Mike's got so busy. This meant less time worrying.

He had noticed a positive change since landing the job at Mike's because it forced him to get himself out of bed and earn money to put towards the rent and necessities like food and electricity, which all previously rested on Taylor's taxable earnings and his own miniscule universal credit income. He was having regular sex with Taylor that he enjoyed and consented to. Swallowing his boyfriend's sperm was now something he looked forward to. However, the existential threat of whether he would go home and have an argument with Taylor always dwelled in the back of his mind like a ticking time bomb. Some days he would be working, taking orders, and then an inner dialogue with his demons would start. He was unsure what triggered the anxiety in him. Callum knew it was unwarranted but once he entered the rabbit hole of worry; it was hard to get out of – which led to incorrect orders, food needing replacing, and poor customer satisfaction.

'Come on, mate. You need to have your head screwed on because they can easily replace you in here. I'm guessing by the hours increase that you need this job. Just giving you a warning because he was *not* happy today,' Michelle had said to him.

Michelle Mitchell was 54 years old and had worked at Mike's for three years since she left her previous job as a cleaner. 'Horrible. I would rather be hung, drawn and quartered than ever clean for anyone again. You would scrub the floors for half an hour and then someone would tread their dirty shoes all over the floor whilst you had the mop still in your hand,' Michelle had said to Callum about her decision to leave her past field of expertise. She spoke matter-of-factly and the years of looking after her three adult boys as a single mother – two were now in prison for GBH and drug charges – had taken its toll on her face. She looked no younger than 65 and had a hoarse throat from years of excessive smoking, tattooed eyebrows and more tacky art – butterflies and stars and her sons' names – down her arms that were barely covered by her uniform.

He knew that she meant Alan, the manager of Mike's, was not happy with him making human errors. If Alan could, he would only employ robots at the chip shop for optimal efficiency. Alan was a short fat man with the angry temperament to match his Napoleon complex; like a Chihuahua you could hear barking down the street at a Great Dane triple its size. Although he was quick to give him a job, two people had already been dismissed within a month. One of them was Fiona – a pretty maths student from Bristol who worked part-time to cover some of her university outgoings – who was sacked for taking longer than 20 seconds to wrap and bag an order.

The End is Near

The 19th was a closing shift for Callum, leaving only him and Michelle to tidy up, clean the equipment, and close Mike's for the night. After completing their chores in silence, she jerked the rusty shutters down so hard that they made an ear-splitting noise, lit her cigarette, and walked in the opposite direction to where Callum was headed without saying goodbye.

Another positive was that it was located on a street next to a hairdressers and newsagents only a ten minute walk from home (seven if he wanted to get home as quick as possible), which meant less travel time to get home to Taylor after a long day of being surrounded by the stench of fish and salt and pepper seasoning.

He stopped on his journey home and fondled in his coat pocket for a cigarette. Retrieving one from the packet, he lit and inhaled a long drag, feeling the recognisable and pleasant effects of nicotine travelling through his body. He continued to walk in thought about his partner and the future they would have together. Living in a house of their own, holidaying five times a year up the Amalfi Coast, expensive clothes, a cute terrier dog. It was all fantasy, but they would make it happen: together. He took the last drag of his cigarette and flicked it away; a gust of cold winter air blew it down the street, the golden spark of what remained descending out of his vision.

The first thing that he felt on entering the flat was the heat. It hit him in the face like a ton of bricks and the noise he had heard from outside was Christmas music, *Last Christmas* by *Wham!*, and Taylor singing the words loudly.

'Cal, is that you? Don't come in here,' Taylor said. 'I said don't fucking come in here. Don't you listen? I'm busy doing something,' Taylor snarled when Callum opened the door ajar to the living room.

'Jesus, okay. What are you doing?'

'Santa is wrapping your fucking presents, so don't even dare come in here. The tea is cooked. Spaghetti Bolognese – I know it's one of your favourites. I'll do you a bowl soon.' Callum's heart warmed. The concept of Taylor floating around the tiny square kitchen with Christmas music on made his heart melt. Pots and pans stacked high in the sink; ingredients spread out on the chopping board waiting for the knife; the fragrant aroma of Italy migrating through the flat.

Callum's mood ultimately depended on how his other half was feeling. From imaginary fireworks exploding after erotic sex to sleepless nights after being sexually abused. He escaped his daze and pulled himself away from falling down a black hole of intrusive thoughts and returned to the present moment: where everything was going perfect. His relationship was how he wanted it to be. His soulmate was in the living room wrapping

Christmas presents for him after cooking his favourite food. What more could he want? He wondered what mechanisms inside of the brain warped his reality and sent him down a long route of darkness; an alternative reality forming before his eyes. With his depression, Callum had the power to sit and conjure up the most vivid imaginary scenario in his head; one of death and despair comparable to that of an ancient tragedy.

There was a bag across the room that caught his eye, lined in sleek black matte with a dusty pink bow across the top. He knew instantly when he saw it up close that it housed an expensive gift inside. He turned the bag around and saw that it was from a local jewellers that Callum had window shopped at. Gold rings glistened in the white lighting. Expensive designer watches were fastened around glass boxes. Security men on the door carefully watching everybody that entered the store. Furtively, he carefully observed how the bow was tied on the bag and successfully attempted a similar bow on his shoelace. Solidifying his decision to mischievously open the bag.

He slid onto the bed and folded his legs, carefully unravelling the bow and strings of the bag. He buried his hands in and pulled out a large rectangular box that had been embossed with a personalised message on the front reading, "**To you, love Taylor x**". The sentimental nature made Callum breakdown to tears. Callum lifted the lid from the box and found a gold bracelet inside. Delicately picking the bracelet up from its box, he observed the fine details of it. It was a heavy gold bracelet with a heart entwined between two thin masses of gold string. This is what the outside world didn't see, Callum thought to himself: the thoughtfulness of Taylor.

He rushed to put the bracelet back in its box when Taylor had shouted for dinner, sealing the bow carefully. He thought to himself that he had done a good job of concealing his immoral activities, brought on by experience of wrapping orders at Mike's.

'This smells delicious. Thank you so much,' Callum exclaimed enthusiastically. Planting a large wet kiss on Taylor's cheek.

'Good day at work I'm assuming?' Anxiety made his chest sink inwards. *He knows*, Callum thought. 'You never randomly kiss me anymore. It feels nice.'

'Oh yeah... l-lovely,' Callum lied.

For dessert, Callum decided to force his way down the back of Taylor's throat with his tongue; the enzymes of both parties switched in a passionate affair. Proceeding down his body, he slid his hand down Taylor's shorts, identifying a stiff erection. He removed his own chip shop uniform quickly until lifted and placed gently onto his lap.

'You feel so good inside of me.'

'You feel so good to be inside of.'

As they continued their passionate affair, Callum moved his positioning submissively so that his lover could slide inside of him perfectly. They stayed in the same cradled position until Taylor shot his load; his DNA within his most intimate body part.

'That felt so good,' Callum said afterwards; short of breath from moaning passionately.

'I love you so much.'

'Love you too, Cal.'

The absence of the letter I was something that would usually send Callum's mind into overdrive with anxiety. However, Callum felt too euphoric to care. He knew that he loved him. The bracelet he bought him was enough and no intrusive thought was going to change his reality. He was free to go to bed with a clear heart and mind: uncommon for somebody with chronic depression.

The continuation of the build up to Christmas passed quickly for both of them: one continuous long day. Working late until Christmas Eve, last minute shopping, wrapping, early nights, and cuddles in bed with

Christmas movies. The first two *Home Alone* movies were Callum's favourite, whilst Taylor opted for *Die Hard* which always started the age-old debate of whether it even constituted a Christmas movie.

'I understand it's not a traditional Christmas movie, but it is one. It's literally set at a Christmas party.'

Everything was perfect when they both woke to the ringing alarm clock on Christmas morning. Christmas of 2023 would be the most perfect day of their relationship. The curtains were left open overnight; the darkness ensuing no illumination crept in whilst they slept. They decided against snoozing their alarms. Taylor switched on the lamp to the side of him, but it failed to light the darkness of the room with its dullness.

'Merry Christmas to you, Cal. Let's have the best day ever.'

'Merry Christmas, Tay. I hope you like your presents. I love you lots.'

'I've got the best present right in front of me.'

Callum felt pure happiness. He had been clean from drugs for over three weeks and the strenuous routine of working long hours had meant that his mind had typically been occupied beyond the realms of drug taking to cure his insomnia, depression, anxiety, or boredom. Today was going to be a perfect day, their first Christmas together as they decided to spend the year before separate because they were not officially together. The flat was excruciatingly humid, condensation rippled down all of the windows in the flat from the bedroom through to the kitchen. Once out of bed, Callum retrieved two mugs from the kitchen cupboard whilst he counted how many presents lay on the floor in the living room – 29 in total. 15 for him wrapped in brown paper flooded with gingerbread men and candy canes, and 14 for Taylor that were wrapped in black wrapping paper with white polar bears printed across.

He looked at his presents from Taylor on one side of the room but couldn't locate the black jewellers' bag. He started to worry. 'Stop worrying, Callum. He's probably hiding it as a surprise.' Callum tried all he could to not let his mental health ruin a day like Christmas when he had worked so hard to make it perfect. The music was thumping out of the radio in the kitchen whilst he made coffee and fried eggs for breakfast in bed.

The plan was for them to go to Taylor's parents' for their dinner – he had already pre-warned Callum that it would be a long night on alcohol with the family; his aunt and uncle were attending along with their two older children and their partners, one of whom had a baby of their own. In total, a group of 11 around a table that only fit six. Theoretically, it was doomed from the start. Informed that there would be heated discussions on politics, sexuality, gender, war, religion, and pop culture, Callum was prepared to keep his mouth firmly closed on topics or they would never return home without settling the debate in the other party's favour.

Although Callum rarely saw the in-laws because of their strained relationship with Taylor, they had accepted him as one of their own. Taylor's parents usually text him at least once a week to check on how he was doing and recently, whether he was prepared for Christmas. Taylor's mum, Pauline, knew how her son's moods could deteriorate rapidly and that he could become aggressive. Callum never had it in him to damage their relationship more so although he appreciated the curiosity, he passed on the offer of exposing the occasional sexual abuse.

Whilst they eat their breakfast in bed – 'I love this. What a great morning,' Taylor had said – the TV was playing *Britain's Favourites: The Top 20 Christmas Songs Voted by You!*

They shared one final kiss, Callum watching the silhouette of Taylor's naked body as he dressed. In his eyes, he was sculpted by the gods. He continued watching in awe, his usual attire of shorts and no t-shirt, grey moccasin slippers lined with cream fur that Callum had bought him out of his first payslip from Mike's. The excitement he felt when he had enough money to buy him a small gift in reward for feeding his drug and alcohol addiction for months. Taylor was ecstatic with the slippers and they had amazing sex that night, he remembered. He hoped that the presents he bought for Christmas would invoke the same joyous response.

To conclude the unwrapping of gifts, Callum had bought Taylor; socks, boxer shorts, two pairs of pyjamas (shorts not pants), far-too-much chocolate, designer inspired shower gels he found on a local Instagram page, a new razor, a pair of jeans, a The North Face tracksuit, a pair of Nike trainers, two Nike t-shirts, a lighter, the trip on the steam-engine train, a gift voucher for £100 to get a new tattoo, and a £150 gift card.

'You shouldn't have spent this much on me, Callum. Thank you so much. I am made up with everything, honestly. Love you, mate. Merry Christmas.' Callum managed a smile; the anxiety knotting his stomach painfully. Anxious that he had betrayed him by rummaging through the bedroom and finding it early. Fear that the expression on his face would give it away, ultimately causing an argument. He dragged his presents over one by one from underneath the window so he could be sat, nervous that his legs may cave in if he stood from the floor.

The first presents he opened were ones of his expectations – socks, underwear, deodorant, and confectionary. The electric razor for "sensitive and intimate areas" felt more like a gift to himself because he always complained that he disliked hair growing on Callum's childlike body. He opened the rest of his presents which included new clothes, trainers, money, and the collection of Harry Potter books from one to seven. However, there was no bracelet in sight. Taylor made another coffee which highlighted that the gift opening had concluded and there were none further to be opened.

In his head, Callum conceptualised ways to ask if there were any forgotten presents without being too direct. 'I'm just trying to think if I have given you everything or if I have forgotten anything. Let me just go and check in the bedroom.'

'Oh, lucky me... receiving potentially more presents. I made sure I checked last night and this morning so you've had all yours.' When the words escaped Taylor's lips, Callum had to run to the bathroom in order to regurgitate his breakfast into the sink. The pain of his throw-ups was excruciating, a burning sensation inside of his stomach that felt like his intestines were attempting to escape his body. He had now realised that he would never be worthy enough, not even for his own boyfriend, someone he had spent almost every day with for nearly a year and a half.

The real question was – who had Taylor bought the gift for? He was aware that infidelity had occurred in the past, he accepted that out of pity and understanding. He once struggled to look after himself which meant he never attended to Taylor's physiological needs. The sex had dried up, Callum's meltdowns were out of control, the drug addiction was draining their bank, and he slept until late evenings. However, that was the past and he thought everything was going well in their relationship because there had only been minor disagreements and the sex seemed extraordinary – so what was it lacking that meant Taylor was not satisfied enough with their relationship? Callum cried silent tears that travelled down his cheeks and plummeted onto the bathroom sink, dampening his skin to the colour of chalk. He needed his boyfriend to survive and his heart shattered that in his entirety, he would never be good enough. His needy personality had proved to be a vital mechanism in the destruction of his own fairy tale ending; rather than blaming Taylor's infidelity for being the cause.

He tried to wipe his tears away but his hands were not strong enough to change his complexion. His skin had turned from pale white to scarlet, blotchy skin around his neck from crying, and puffy eyes that made him look unwell.

Callum attempted to retrace their schedules but couldn't think of a time other than at work when they had been apart. They had been shopping together, out for walks, coffee, the cinema, and drinking with Stacey on the day before Christmas Eve. Panic galloped around his insides that his boyfriend's body had potentially lay entangled with somebody else. But what if it hadn't? What if it was a surprise? A simple misunderstanding? he thought to himself.

'What are you doing in there? Your coffee is going to be fucking freezing. You have been gone for ages.'

'Sorry. I have been tidying about in here. Thank you for the drink, let me just finish up in here and I'll be back through.'

'Okay, but hurry up. I need a piss,' Taylor said.

They arrived home to a cold flat just after three o'clock in the morning, intoxicated by alcohol and exhausted from all of the food they had eaten throughout the day. His parents had served them with more breakfast when they arrived at their cosy home – a full English with mini croissants – and a beautiful roast dinner.

He met Taylor's extended family and they all shared an interest in wanting to know more about him, his education, family dynamic, career, and future prospects. It was intimidating at times to discuss himself but they soothed his anxiety with anecdotes of their lives, working class Liverpool in the 1960s, and remaining calm when he stumbled on his words. They had also watched Christmas specials on TV, danced around the living room, played board games – they opted out of Monopoly due to time constraints – and ranted about the government and the latest celebrity gossip. On the face of it, the day was perfect, but the dread of infidelity lurked over the house like a curse. Smiling was paired with blank expressions; warmness turned dull; satisfaction turned to hostility.

'Tay, I'm tired. I'm not really in the mood for sex,' Callum admitted. 'Please, I really can't be bothered,' he said again when Taylor continued to try and initiate love-making.

'Stop being boring and let me fuck you.'

'No. Fucking listen to me! Taylor, I really don't want to have sex tonight!'

'What the fuck is wrong with you? We have had a lovely night. Why end it so abruptly?'

Now's your only chance, Callum thought to himself. Be truthful. Be brave. Be understanding.

'Where's the bracelet?' He didn't possess the strength to turn his body around but he felt Taylor's body jolt up when he asked the question.

'What are you talking about? What bracelet?'

'The one in the black bag with a heart on. I saw the bag in here when I finished work the other night and you were wrapping my stuff in the living room. You didn't do a very good job at hiding it, so I opened it, and it was from you. Don't lie because your name was engraved on the box, so where is it?'

'I have no idea what you are talking about, Callum,' Taylor said.

'Oh, please. Stop trying to make me look like a fucking *idiot*. There was a gold bracelet in this bedroom and now it has gone. Where is it?'

'I… ummm… took it to my mum's the other day for her to hide… because I didn't want you to find it. Yeah, silly me, I left it there. What am I like?' Taylor laughed.

Callum sniggered to himself, 'you are a liar. You haven't been to your mum's recently and you didn't take a bag around with you today. Wow. Just tell me the truth.'

'You're so fucking weird, Callum. I'm not lying, I've just fucking told you! Number one; you shouldn't have been creeping around my shit like it has anything to do with you. Number two; I did in fact buy that fucking bracelet for you but because you are such an overthinking little freak you have ruined it now. Number three; don't ever call me a fucking liar again when I haven't lied about anything!'

Taylor could hear the noise of Callum's phone unlocking as he lay next to him in the bed.

'Hey, Pauline, sorry to call you so late… I know you are probably in bed… but has Taylor left a present in yours by any chance? It is sealed up in a black bag,' Callum muttered through the phone, 'oh, he didn't? Okay… no worries then, it must be here somewhere. Thanks anyways. Thanks for a lovely day and a lovely dinner. Have a nice sleep, sorry to wake you. Thanks, will do. Love you too, Pauline.'

'How *fucking dare* you. How fucking dare you phone my mum at this hour to ask her a fucking question like that? How fucking dare you, Callum!'

'*Liar*. I fucking knew it. I can't do this anymore. I am done with you.'

'Oh, just fucking go then, Callum! It's not as if I even want you here, anyway. Just fucking *get out*,' Taylor said aggressively, scrolling through Instagram on his phone as he spoke.

'Cal, I'm sorry. It was nothing, I bought it for you but then I lost it. I promise you. I'm not lying now.'

Taylor sat in bed, continuously talking but receiving no response from Callum who rapidly moved through the bedroom, turbulently dressing himself back into the clothes that he had discarded on the floor. A hoodie, jeans, Vans.

Before he could expand his lie any further; Callum was out of the flat, running down the stairs, and running down the road. He had no idea where he was running to but knew he had to run away from life. He wondered whether Wendy's was an option, but it was Christmas Day night turned Boxing Day morning and he opted against waking her and the boys up. He knew that Agnes would never accept him back at her home. Alone he was.

He had lost everything to him. Friendships had broken-down; his future was dilapidated; his brain in turmoil. He was finished with the self-doubt endured. He wanted the old Callum back. The one free of him. He knew since Taylor that he had transformed to a toxic entity: one of nothing but sadness and regret.

To be on his own, to fend for himself, to strive for greatness, is what he needed to do.

The End is Near

CHAPTER FIVE

Callum

'The night I left him was Christmas Day. Well, early hours Boxing Day. I found out that he had given a lovely bracelet to somebody else. He was cheating on me, basically. I think it hurt me more because it was from a shop that he knew I've *always* dreamt of owning something from. It was a gorgeous bracelet as well… he did have good taste. Ha.' Callum intended the comment as a joke but realised that it sounded serious.

'A gold one it was, with a heart in the middle of it. And I was delusional enough to think that he had bought it for me. He hadn't. He said he did when I confronted him but I knew it was for somebody else when his mum confirmed it, so I ran out of the flat that night and that's why I have ended up here. I slept on the street for a night, a few miles away from my old childhood home. I knocked at my nan's house at about seven in the morning. I knew she always got up early. She wouldn't let me in. Luckily, someone told me to come here which is why I am here with you. Wow, I could never be homeless again, touch wood. My heart breaks for them. It was a terrifying experience… and *so* fucking cold. I've never felt as low in my life than when I slept in a freezing cold wet park. I needed that freedom to understand what was going on in my head.'

'Wait, Callum. Can we please just go back to the beginning for a second. You said that you found a bracelet from him but it wasn't a gift for you? How can you be sure it wasn't for you?' Ed, his therapist of two sessions, asked.

Following running away from home, Callum had been placed on the list for emergency psychological support offered by the hostel where he had ended up. His positive relationship with the hostel staff meant that he was sifted from the queue quickly and three weeks later, his first session with Edward – or Ed as he liked to be called – commenced. Ed was in his mid 30s with thick brown hair, a quiff hairstyle except one curled lock that draped from the scalp like Clark Kent pre-Superman costume change. The hairstyle and brown round glasses gave him a quintessential nerdy look but his dark chest hair that protruded from his shirt and thick muscles made Callum wonder what he could look like underneath his clothes. He imagined that he had a sixpack, firm pecs, and thick muscular calves from weight training and running twice a week. His pants hid thick thighs and a tight bulge that Callum struggled to avoid eye contact with. Especially because he sat with his legs wide open: discussing vulnerable topics.

'Because it said it was from him and I never received it on Christmas Day. I even pretended that I'd forgotten one of his presents and went looking for it. I looked for the bag and couldn't find it. He said he was leaving it for after Christmas and was going to give it to me then. I called his mum and asked if he left a bag there, which is what he told me, and she said no. Then he carried on lying to me so I left.'

'But still – how do you know for certain? It seems that the negative outcome was all that you excepted and maybe he could have been telling the truth? I don't know, though. This is something we need to work on whilst you are under my care. Your anxiety and negative view of yourself.' Ed also had mesmerisingly blue eyes that looked at you with no judgement.

'I get that… I suppose. But he wouldn't have given the bracelet to me because it was never intended for me. He hasn't found me, I'm not sure how he would, but I just want to forget about him and try and get back on track for myself.' Callum felt his bottom lip quiver in an attempt to fight back tears at the thought of a life without him, because no matter how angry he was, it terrified him that he could live life without his first love.

'Okay, so if we assume that this bracelet was for you and you hadn't found it that night. If he gave it to you on Christmas Day, how do you think you would be feeling now?'

'Wow. I don't know, to be honest with you. I have never thought about it like that.'

He felt enclosed in the small pale room simply decorated with two black leather sofas and tacky motivational quotes hung crooked in a frame above Ed's head that read, **"YOUR MENTAL HEALTH IS JUST AS IMPORTANT AS YOUR PHYSICAL HEALTH"** and the one to his left read **"HELP IS OUT THERE"** in purple font. The room seemed like a black hole that sucked existence away rather than a safe space aimed at recovery. The only thing in the office that seemed symbolic of redemption was Ed and his beauty.

'I think I would be happy because he got me something I really wanted… ummm… I think I would still be overthinking and feeling anxious about our relationship.'

'What makes you assume you would still feel anxious? I know I am probably asking you too many questions, so apologies. I don't want to feel like I'm pressuring you to answer anything. Nonetheless, I need to know the full timeline of your relationship to unpick your thought processes and what I can do to change your outlook before we discuss other things,' Ed replied with intense eye contact.

'Okay, thanks. I understand. Sorry, this will take me a while to be as open as you want. There is a lot I would like to get off my chest so I hope

I do build the confidence to let it out to you.' They managed a smile at one another.

'We will go at your own pace. It may take five sessions, or fifty sessions, but I want to get to a point where I feel as though a burden has been lifted off of your shoulders and you can freely talk to me about anything that gets you down, or any past trauma that feeds into your depression and anxiety, or even just your trivial thoughts about the weather.'

'Thanks, Ed. What was I even talking about? S-sorry... I've forgotten.' Callum felt piping hot. He couldn't believe how beautiful Ed was. Light freckles covered his nose.

'No need to apologise. You were saying that you would still feel anxious even if the bracelet had been gifted to you? I asked why you feel as though you would be anxious. Please, do take your time. There is no rush.' However, there was a rush, Callum thought to himself. They only had one hour per session and over 35 minutes had already been used, discussing nothing of value.

'Yeah so... I think I would still be anxious because deep down... I know I couldn't trust him 100% of the time. I've never admitted that before, so it feels strange to say. I loved him... and... I still do. However, I knew he had cheated on me in the past. I had caught him and allowed it because I wanted the relationship to work so much that I thought him having sex with other people would keep both of us happy. In conclusion, it was only him who stayed happy. I thought that if he had better sex elsewhere, he would come back and love me after it. S-sorry, Ed. I feel weird talking about my sex life with you.'

'Please, Callum. Do not apologise. I want to know how you are feeling and if that means diving deep into your sex life, then I suppose that is necessary, albeit rather intrusive. You need to stop apologising for getting things off of your chest. I shouldn't really be saying this but I can assure you now that I have heard a lot worse than what you are about to tell me.' Ed managed a polite smile and a long gulp of his coffee. Callum watched the Adam's apple roll inside of his neck when he drank, feeling a burning desire to kiss him – aware of how inappropriate that thought was.

'I find having sex *very* vulnerable. When he cheated again, I knew that it was my fault because I could not give him what he wanted. I thought that there must be something wrong with me and I was stupid enough to think that if I changed my ways, it would be different. We still had intercourse even when I found out that he had cheated on me. We were always experimenting with new things to do – the sex was never boring. S-sorry, Ed… that was far too much information.'

'Callum, please stop apologising.'

'Sorry. Sorry. It's a habit. I realised that if I couldn't give him what he wanted, it was obviously a fault with who I am as a person.'

'That is exactly the reason why you need to be here with me. Someone has been unfaithful to you and your belief system is that there is an issue within yourself rather than an issue with him for cheating on you. Statistics have shown that in gay relationships, one of the main reasons for infidelity is personal insecurities. I can promise you now, Callum, that it has got nothing to do with who you are as a person. People can be unfaithful in relationships because they have endured trauma from previous relationships or things in their childhood that have impacted how they perceive themselves, which obviously leads to low self-esteem, hatred, and commitment issues. My point is that he failed to see what he had in front of him when you seem like a respectable young lad who is polite, articulate, and kind. Just because your ex-partner failed to see all of the positives in what your relationship was doesn't mean that it was your fault, at all. This to me is a key indicator that your ex-partner was actually not okay. People put a mask on in fear of being vulnerable or that people may think less of them because they have an illness.'

Callum watched as Ed uncrossed his legs and wiggled around in his seat, but never took his eyes off him when he spoke. He noted that all therapists he had seen in movies all had the same monotone-yet-charismatic approach to their practice, stern expressions with undertones of condescendence.

'So, when you felt the low points of your relationship, how did you cope with this? Did you have a method that maybe numbed your pain or distracted your mind?' Ed asked.

'Ummm... I'm just trying to think, give me a second.' He was unsure whether it would be normal to discuss his meltdowns or substance abuse issues on the second session, or whether he should even mention it at all. He knew that he had grown out of drugs. However, he never wanted Ed to think of him as a druggie when used as a form of medication in a past life; just as the Victorians had used arsenic for asthma or cancer.

'I honestly can't think of anything... ummm... let me think. I-I think I would just zone out and go about my day as normal. I was out of a job for months, so yeah... not much. Sorry.'

'Okay. So you just suppressed all of your emotions down as if they were irrelevant. You need to put yourself first and feel things deeply because suppressing emotions down could lead to things building up which eventually leads to chronic depression, or dysthymia, if you would like the medical term. Do you not have anyone you have spoken to about things in the past?'

'I suppose. Wendy was one of my neighbours down the road from us and she was the nicest woman ever who gave me great advice and always left me feeling better. Then I had my nan… but we're no longer on speaking terms.'

Callum recited the story with his grandmother and received swift nodding from Ed who listened to every word without interruption. Ed recommended that he attempted to reconnect with Agnes, Callum told him that he had failed in his quest of rekindling their relationship and didn't want to try again. Furthermore, he eventually told Ed that he was reliant on Class A substances and marijuana. 'I was on them near enough every single day for over a year. I would wake up so late because I didn't have a job to go to because I got sacked from my last one and then I would just roam around like a zombie until Taylor got home from work and then we would get back on drugs until all hours in the morning.'

'We both know the impact drugs can have on our mental and physical health, so it is excellent that you no longer take them and I hope you stick with sobriety, Callum. I really do. The reason you probably feel so emotional at this moment is because we are having a deep conversation about your past, also because your body is purging from the drugs and if you were taking them so regularly, it will take a while for them to completely flush out of your system. This can lead to erratic mood swings from happy, to sad, to anxiety, to optimism. If you persevere through the storm, you will make it out the other end, I promise you. I'm here to guide you and help you understand the way you are feeling and how you can manage your depression so that it doesn't take over your life. I want you to flourish. It will take a while. It all starts with you taking control of your life and the path you want to go down, okay?'

As the session drew to a close, Ed tasked Callum with a piece of homework to complete in time for their next session. He asked Callum to write down what he was grateful for, what triggered his anxiety, why he wanted to remain single, and where he saw himself in five years.

'See you soon, Ed.'

'Bye, Callum. Take care of yourself. Get as deep as you want with what I have tasked you with. That is what I'm here for,' Ed said with a charismatic smile.

Callum had been fired from Mike's for not attending his shifts on numerous occasions and was jobless for a short-but-felt-like-a-lifetime period of staying at the hostel; having no fixed abode a difficulty to get back into employment. The hostel was called Helpful Hand Initiative (it got abbreviated to HHI; pronounced as hi) and was located in the city centre of Liverpool.

His dedication to pursuing a life of happiness motivated him to apply for more jobs, with many rejections, but within 20 days he had been employed in Primark, a multinational fashion retailer, as a retail assistant.

The End is Near

They called Callum to tell him that he had secured the job within two hours of interview and his training had commenced the Monday after. In his interview, he told the interviewing panel – that consisted of the store manager and an independent recruiter from outside the business – facts about Primark he found from Wikipedia, how he could minimise risk to consumers, steps to negate excess stock, and how he had previous experience working as part of a team. He accepted the job contentedly.

Feeling alone had left him motivated and aspirational. He was still living in the hostel whilst working at Primark but he had been promised by Ian – the manager of HHI – that he could stay there until he had a deposit for a place to rent and was still under Ed's care. He wasn't sure whether Ian felt obliged to allow him to stay there – a form of pity for how much of an imbecile he was being young, homeless, heartbroken, and queer – but somewhere deep inside he thought that Ian may have actually liked him for whom he was. Ian was also homosexual and had told him that he always invested time in his own queer community because he saw a fragment of himself in young gays because his own life could have panned out the same if he never had the right support system in place. Ian kept him up to date with all of the new LGBTQIA+ (he never missed the QIA+) news stories in the world, what celebrities had worn at the latest awards show, and his Jack Russell at home named Jasper who seemed to urinate in the house more than outside in the park. Callum strangely felt like he had made a friend in Ian the more time that he spent with him.

As the weeks rolled on and their friendship grew more intense, Ian said something to him one night in what was classed as the communal living room that consisted of nothing more than an archaic TV as wide as a coffin, three long brown leather sofas that reminded him of the one that was in the flat the first time he met Taylor, and a handful of paintings on the walls; a bowl of fruit, a picturesque cliff with a lonely house as the centrepiece, a man and woman abstractly drawn naked, among others.

'Callum, I'm not meant to say things like this but if you ever want to go for a drink or if you want to take my number and we can chat, just let me know. I class you as my friend now, to be honest with you. You're a cracker; proper sound lad,' Ian had said.

Ian was 36 years old and had been the manager of the hostel for three years, having previously worked as a social worker, with a master's in Social Work from Manchester Met and a bachelor's degree in Cognitive Psychology from Liverpool Hope. He was bald with ginger stubble, tall, and quite handsome in an unusual way, crooked teeth and a thin nose, large nostrils attached to the bottom.

The weeks rolled by as the therapy sessions intensified, his responsibilities at work expanded further than the job description stated, and he continued to browse for one-bedroom flats to rent within his budget. He liked the magnitude of pressure. Callum believed he was switching back to who he once was. Someone with drive that burned inside of him like a melted flame. He opened up more to Ed by explaining his childhood trauma, his past relationship with Taylor, his abandonment issues, and his low self-esteem. It was daunting to be vulnerable to a random stranger who happened to be one of the most beautiful men on the planet, but if eye contact was avoided and enough coffee was had, he could.

Hey mate, I know you're in work but I just thought I'd ask ya. Me, Jay and Kate are going for our quiz night tonight in the Blue Herring in town if you fancy coming with us. We could do with your pointless knowledge ha-ha – let me know if you're up for it. We'll be having a few too mate!

It was a Thursday in late February at work when Ian had text him, checked on his lunchtime walk through the city centre. Teenagers in school uniforms blowing large clouds of smoke from disposable vapes; religious preaches of Christianity, Islam, and Judaism preaching about their God all within thirty yards of one another; drunks singing *American Pie* on the karaoke. Liverpool was at its best. After everything he had been tasked to complete during the rest of his shift, the thought of a crisp glass of wine whilst answering puzzling questions he would never need the answers for sounded appealing. He was excited to meet Jay and Kate, whomever they may be.

From the evil received over the past year, maybe leaving Taylor was needed for happiness. Being in a relationship to experience life wholly was illogical. Happiness could be found in the little things: meeting new people; building platonic relationships; fresh pastries; discovering a new singer and their discography; drinking modestly at pub quizzes. He crawled through the remainder of his shift; sorting the deliveries of inventory that came from the warehouse; working the tills; adjusting the floor; answering customer queries.

Natalie Smith was amusing but not somebody that Callum would entertain outside of the workplace. She was aggressive, illiterate, loose-lipped, and confrontational. Her attire consisted of tatty hair extensions that never matched her natural hair colour, false eyelashes, over pumped lips, and streaky false tan.

'Cal, I've just been in the staffroom and Daniel wants a word with you. He wants you now, he said. Told me to come and take over whatever you are doing so you could go. Cheeky fat fuck. I told him I was heading on my break and then he started ranting that I'm not entitled to smoking breaks. I told him I am entitled to them breaks or I will go insane, the daft bastard.' Callum winced at Natalie's comment and headed through the shop, making his way down two flights of escalators to the back of the building where the staffroom was located, passing rows of stockrooms stuffed with cheap stock made in sweat shops in foreign countries, the most expensive priced at £55 for a long wool coat.

In the staffroom, the stout manager Daniel sat at the table with another senior colleague Anita. The first thing he noticed of Daniel was his posture – how curved his spine was because of his enormous potbelly that failed him to be no closer than five inches away from the table. He had thin strands of brown hair on his scalp and a pale, rough complexion. The room's air conditioning left an icy chill in the air but he noticed droplets of sweat formed at the sides of Daniel's forehead above his temples. He wiped his forehead when he saw that Callum had entered the room; muting the conversation with slender Anita who left on cue. He struggled to think of any issues he brought to Primark since commencing employment – punctual, driven, exceptional communication skills, and always helped customers, so much so that he had formal compliments from customers.

'Good afternoon, Callum. I hope you're feeling well today. I'm assuming that you know the reason I have called you in here today?' Daniel asked, wiping his head with the palm of his chubby right hand.

'Nope, I have no idea.'

'Callum, you must know that I have noticed the work that you do. I know I'm *extremely* busy as the manager. Ha. However, I do notice things that go on. Your work ethic is phenomenal. You go above and beyond for this company and to have written compliments in from customers is something unheard of, most especially for someone of your young age. You are an impeccable employee – by far the best I have ever employed. You aren't afraid to try anything; you know how to do almost everything in here; all of the other staff have nothing but nice things to say about you. So yes, I called you in here for a quick catch up and to thank you for your hard work.'

'Thank you so much. That means a lot,' Callum managed a smile.

'No worries, mate. However… I'm not sure if you had heard the news. I'm assuming you haven't if you have no idea why you're in here. I'm sadly leaving in a couple of weeks because I have been promoted to area manager for Merseyside – I've been going for interviews and tests since the start of December. Normally, we would put a job post out for my job but it can be done internally if we feel as though somebody meets the criteria. So, really, what I'm asking is, would you please do me the biggest favour of my life and become the store manager here? It should save me so much time on recruitment and interviewing people. I know it's not the best place to work… it's constantly messy, full of thieves, and you are probably looking for something else more intellectually stimulating… it could do for the time being. It would be a pay rise and more opportunity to build your skills.'

The End is Near

Callum – shockingly – cried when offered the job. He never imagined himself to be someone with managerial traits, so accepting it was a worry. He felt immensely proud that he was capable of achieving the feat without even having to apply. Strangely, when he accepted the role as store manager, the first thought in his mind was what Taylor could be doing and whether he would be proud of him. Would he be at work today or was it his day off from the wholesalers? Would he be having sex with somebody else or could he be masturbating imagining the sex that they used to have?

Getting rid of Taylor had seemed to open a gateway to success – not allowing his mind to be demonised by something so cancerous. The duration of his shift ticked over fast and he couldn't wait to get back "home" – emergency accommodation shared with 35 other people fleeing poverty, domestic violence, and addiction issues – to tell Ian the news of his promotion.

When he arrived back, Ian was already waiting at the reception desk with a girl in her 30s with fiery ginger hair and freckles all over her face and arms. She wore a large, black, vintage oval hat, a short-sleeved cream dress with bright red strawberries printed on, sheer tights underneath, and a pair of Doc Martens. She was very pretty, Callum thought, with an aura that exuded warmth and kindness, like Ian.

'Look! Here he is finally. Callum, Kate. Kate, Callum. Jay's not coming now, "under the weather" he said.'

Kate rose from one of two orange sofas that were known to be the waiting area at the front of the accommodation; a squelch emerging underneath as she peeled her body from the worn leather.

'Hello love!' Kate pulled him close for a warm hug. 'I've heard lots about you. God, I'm sorry to hear that you're staying here. When Ian told me he made a friend in the hostel I thought the worst. *Sorry*. I didn't mean anything bad about you! All strange fuckers walk through these doors… I thought he may have befriended an undercover axe murderer on the run.'

'I possibly could be an axe murderer. You never know,' Callum joked.

Opening the door to his private bedroom with nothing but a single bed with faded white cotton sheets, a cracked wooden headboard surrounded by faded pistachio coloured walls, and a single thin clothing rail that struggled to fit even half of the clothes that lined the floors in binbags bought with his discount at Primark, was reality for Callum.

Whilst getting dressed for quiz night, Callum thought of what the wage increase would mean to him. The additional £400 a month could be put towards a deposit for a rental flat of his own; somewhere in the city centre close to his current location. He liked the accessibility of everything he wanted being within a half mile radius: work; restaurants; shops; bars; parks; the waterfront. He liked the bustling crowds that passed his windows shouting football chants when the local teams had won their games; the laughing of girlfriends drunk on wine; the noise of the birds tweeting in the morning; the howl of the wind as the season approached spring. He liked to imagine that he was in New York or Paris, a popular socialite with bustles of crowds waiting outside his hotel suite for a glimpse of his beauty. Other times, his anxiety crept in whilst trying to sleep and reality would hit him that he was living in a hostel surrounded by crack fiends who just wanted a place of warmth for one night before they went back out begging for money in the bleak weather, chasing the dragon to alleviate themselves from their gruesome reality, and completing unspeakable tasks at the hands of drug lords for small cash. When Callum had these thoughts, he wished for nothing more than to be with Agnes, who did all she could to protect him from the harsh side of his home city.

That evening, Callum decided to wear a black knitted sweater that stuck to his body in an irritable way, skinny washed jeans he purchased for £6 from the clearance dump at work, and black Nike trainers.

Though the hostel had its flaws, living rent-free was something he would never complain about.

He discarded his dirty uniform in the wash basket located at the bottom of the hall and made his way downstairs. He could see a congregation of addicts outside of the hostel door, smoking cigarettes and likely in discussions of how they would fund their next fix. It confused him why so many had the opportunity to stay in the warmth of the hostel but still chose to sleep on the streets or wander round until all hours of the morning: cold, destitute, off their heads.

'My manager called me in today,' Callum opened the conversation to Ian and Kate. It had only taken him five rapid minutes to get ready.

'And?'

'We had a chat.'

'Yeah, about what, Callum? Don't try and drag this out for the suspense. I have a Psychology degree so you can't play them mind games on me.'

'He is leaving to become the area manager… and I've been asked to become the new store manager! I could cry; well I did cry right in front of him and I felt so embarrassed. I am so happy with myself!' Ian spun Callum in circular motions until vomit was at the forefront of his mouth. He plastered a friendly kiss on his cheek, making both of them blush.

'Wow! Well done, Cal. No one deserves it more than you. You should be so proud of yourself. However, on the contrary, I'm not too happy myself... because this means you're finally growing up like my own little child and you're going to be out of here soon.'

'Thank you for everything you have done for me. I think you still have a bit more time with me, though. Friends for life – pinkie promise?' Callum said, raising his little finger. The promise was accepted.

'Right, let's go and get drunk.'

The three of them headed out of the hostel and made their way to The Blue Herring, half a mile yonder. The boozer was marketed as an indie pub – nestled between a newsagents and a brunch spot – with turquoise and white glossy painting across the perimeter of the building. A cartoon blue herring hung above the doorway, submerged to the naked eye in enchanting flora. Callum imagined the pub should be plotted in Notting Hill, or Antibes, rather than down a seedy avenue in Liverpool city centre where the passers-by were drunken idiots or people who never appreciated the design of the pub because they were too busy looking at their phones. The pub was fairly loud inside, Kate managed to get a table nestled away in the corner that gave a sense of privacy. The floors were dark oak and the walls were painted a warm white that allowed the hundreds of paintings and antiques hung from the walls and shelves to be the essence of the building. The clientele were diverse, ranging from barely legal adults to over 60s, high heels to trainers, tracksuits to flowy dresses, and extensions to bald heads. It felt snug to be in The Blue Herring, a feeling of unity amongst the attendees who worked in conjunction to ensure pathways to the toilets were clear, the queue for the bar was orderly, and the volume inside was minimised for the quiz host to read the questions without unnecessary repetition.

They named themselves *The Three Musketeers* no matter how cliché it seemed, because that is what they felt like that evening – a united trio of swashbuckling heroes, tasked with winning the pub quiz for a cheap bottle of prosecco and chocolates. They laughed until their bellies hurt, drank enough wine to flood a cellar, and danced awkwardly at the table to the faint music that played during the quiz. The atmosphere was electric, eruptions escaped from the crowd when an obscure question was asked and murmurs like a beehive buzzed when teams discussed the possible answers. They finished fourth in the quiz with a score of 27 out of 50.

After The Blue Herring kicked them out just before one o'clock in the morning, the three of them decided on Heaven – one of the only gay nightclubs open until the early hours through the week. The walk was four minutes and the climate was icy; rain pattering against the concrete underneath their feet. The sky was dark grey and the corporate office buildings stood tall above them. In Heaven, the crowd was ecstatic as hot queer men in tight leather rubbed against one another in the discotheque to electrifying techno music, the club illuminated briefly by flashing disco lights. The music playing when they first arrived had no words which provided a sense of anonymity to the club and supplied a state of euphoria for the attendees.

The rainbow colours emitted from the club's lighting resulted in an acute sensitivity to light which made Callum rush to the toilet in order to projectile vomit the alcohol up. Before he could make it to the bathroom, vomit exploded out of Callum's mouth, sliding down the stairs leading to the toilets.

At the sight of what stood before him, the intense feeling of dread overpowered him. His stomach knotted – similar to receiving heart wrenching news.

It was him.

The End is Near

CHAPTER SIX

Taylor

Taylor woke early hours on Boxing Day morning on minimal sleep with a late Christmas gift in the form of throbbing pain all over his body, a consequence of all the alcohol drank the night prior. The unexpected row with Callum never made his hangover any better.

Taylor had a strenuous day ahead on one of the busiest days of the year, the last thing he needed occupying his mind was worrying where that fragile idiot was. He could be roaming the streets on his own, trafficked in the back of a lorry with 40 others, staying at Wendy's or Agnes', or maybe even deceased from a lack of food and water.

He struggled to fathom how a day as serene as Christmas could have ended in such a whirlwind of rage. Callum's ungodly intention to damage a sacred day had been fulfilled. Taylor glugged the remains of lukewarm water, floating particles of food atop; remnants of the day before yesterday's pizza swirling in the plastic bottle. He swallowed two paracetamol and arose like Dracula out of his coffin towards the bathroom to commence his basic hygiene routine. He got a quick rinse under the shower, reciting the previous night's drama in his head. Callum confronting him; the screaming match between the pair; the telephone call with his mother; an expensive gold bracelet.

He made a mental note to check his phone once he was out of the bathroom to see if he had received any texts. As much as he pretended not to care, he did. After completing a warm shower, he wiped his body over with a dirty towel hanging from the corner of the bath; slowly rubbing the tip of his morning glory that pulsated against the cotton. It seemed a shame, he thought, that on the morning of Boxing Day, no one was available to aid his sexual fantasies.

Before Taylor decided to check his phone, he lay naked on the bed, getting irritated by the moisture of the damp towel that grazed against the back of his legs.

Taylor what was all that about last nite??? Callum foning me? Have you been lying to him again? I fucking told u last time. He is a nice lad and you treat him like shit. No respect whatsoever!!! You should be ashamed.

I've text him an had no reply. Tried phonin you 2 and no reply. Is everything ok? Mum.

Two texts he had received from his mother. One from his father.

Call me

Nonetheless, there were zero messages from Callum. He turned his head to the other side of the room and there it was; his phone threw on the floor. He left without his phone. No bank card. No money. Nothing.

'He's going to be okay. Just give him some time,' he mumbled out loud.

Taylor dressed rapidly; his usual work uniform on within two minutes. He headed out the flat with both of his earphones in; *Abbey Road* accompanied him on his journey to Milton's. He noticed the number of cars lined up in the parking bays when he headed into the gates, wondering how sad life must be to visit the wholesaler for discounts on Boxing Day.

The odour of nicotine and sweat in the staffroom was nauseating, an aide-mémoire of the previous nights filled with cheap alcohol and foods high in saturated fats. The smell of cigarettes on clothing was usually soothing for Taylor who enjoyed to smoke but the aroma that day was stomach churning. He edged around the room's perimeter in an attempt to avoid small talk and questions of his day. Within two minutes, he filled both Tommy and Jay in on the entirety of Christmas Day. Their breakfast in bed, the exchange of presents, the food, the ambience at his parents' home, and the departure of Callum following their row. The only detail that Taylor left out – he thought it was too minor to discuss – was the fact he had purchased a bracelet for somebody else that Callum discovered.

Tommy said he was apprehensive that Taylor had not disclosed all of the relevant facts. Jay said that Taylor had nothing to worry about and Callum would be back within a couple of days. He said his goodbyes and headed through to the shop floor.

Before Taylor could get any further to the back of the store, Adrian had obstructed his path like a guard dog, making it impossible to move around him without use of force.

'Wait there a second. Tommy just told me what happened. What have you done now you absolute twat? Merry Christmas for yesterday, too,' Adrian said.

He loved Adrian. A loyal accomplice in and out of work. They laughed together, made plans for the future, and never took life seriously. He was a great boss and never took nonsense from anybody. However, one factor he strongly detested about him was his emotional support for Callum. Whenever the two had a disagreement, it was always Team Callum no matter the circumstances. *Callum smashing plates off his head on drugs?* Taylor must have done something wrong. *Threatening suicide because his gut said he had been cheated on?* Team Callum all the way.

'You say anything bad about what I'm about to tell you and honestly… I know you are my boss… I will punch you in the face. I'm not even joking. I'm in a twat of a mood today. I'm telling you this because I trust you. You're my friend, Adrian.' Adrian held his hands up in a non-threatening way, a sign for Taylor to initiate talks about the night before.

'So he found something he shouldn't have and then phoned my mum at about three in the morning and went psycho. Absolute nutcase he is.' *Why is my voice trembling like that?* Taylor wondered to himself.

'An expensive gold bracelet is what he found. It wasn't a gift for him though. Don't even start, Adrian. It was for someone I've been seeing since about August. Casually, obviously. His name is Liam but I'll fill you in on that another time if you really need to know all of the finer details. Me being stupid left the bag in the bedroom when he was home and he found it. I hid it in the kitchen behind the sink and he realised that it was gone. Don't get me wrong, it's bad to have someone living with me and I'm buying stuff for other people. If it was the other way round; I'd snap his neck. So, I do feel guilty but Callum should never have been snooping around through my stuff. And the way he reacted to it, phoning my mum, that's what annoyed me the most. Then that soft bitch just blurted it all out so now I'm done with her, too. Honestly, I've had a night from hell and now I'm in this shithole for the whole fucking day when I just want to be in bed.'

When Adrian asked Taylor where he had met his new mistress, he confessed they met at a bar in August which resulted in sex in the alleyway and the rest being history, according to Taylor. He was disgusted with his conduct – it had made him think about Lucy, his ex-girlfriend who had been carrying on with another man behind his back. The depression he felt for six months after was scary: he thought that he would never look at women the same again.

The reason emotional infidelity differed was the fact that you shared your heart with somebody. Your likes; dislikes; quirks; idiosyncrasies. As a result, they made a mockery of it, broke your trust, and disposed of the mutual agreement to respect one another, which meant habitual hatred followed suit.

'He is so much more chilled compared to Callum. He knows I live with Callum but that has never bothered him. He says he will wait for me to split up with him. We text all the time, his number is saved under your name. Sorry, Ade. *Ha*. We have good sex, he's funny, but most importantly, he's calm. I don't know why I got myself involved with Callum in the first place; I think I just needed someone to be with, you know. Feeling lonely and wanting someone there all the time,' was Taylor's response when Adrian asked what was different between his partner and his adulterer.

'Okay, I understand that. But I'm sorry to say that isn't the way to go about it. I get what you're saying but you could have fucked Callum off and then found somebody else. Not used both of them at the same time. Then he would've had time to get himself back together and not have to find out about something like that in the way he did.'

After concluding conversations with Adrian confessing distaste for Taylor's behaviour and a firm informal warning not to disrespect his partner again, Taylor continued for the rest of his shift striving to rid everything from his brain what happened the day before. Christmas 2023 had definitely been the worst on record, Taylor thought to himself. The more engrossed he became with work, the more he thought anxiously about Callum, wondering where he was and how he had survived the night on his own.

He knew what he needed after a bank holiday spent at work: rough sex. Rough sex would cure his anxiety, at least for a short period. On his break, he called Liam to arrange plans for that evening.

'I'd like to see you later, Li. I haven't been on my phone for a couple of days – for obvious reasons. Christmas and all that. Just letting you know I'm now single so you can come round whenever you're ready. I will tell you about it later. I have something to give you,' Taylor said.

Liam ended the call without saying goodbye.

Because Liam was visiting, Taylor knew it wouldn't take long before the second most submissive boy in his life would be begging for his body. He put fresh bedding on to make the room as presentable as possible. He discarded cigarette packets, empty water bottles, and dirty plates, but a horrid smell lingered throughout the flat. The smell of dirty washing and sweat. If Callum never returned; living as a single man meant that he could finally decorate the flat as he wanted. Less junk, more wardrobe space, a bed to himself, and paper plates to avoid dish washing.

After a quick shower and masturbation session, a buzzer in the hallway rang – symbolic of Liam's arrival. Taylor opened the front door and observed how Liam strode up the block's stairs with a feminine aura, like Callum's doppelganger. He was around five-foot six with bleached blonde hair, tanned skin as a result of layers of fake tan, a sharp jawline manufactured by non-surgical enhancements, fuzzy eyebrows brushed high on his forehead, and large blue doe eyes. He oozed sex, Taylor thought. A navy bubble coat zipped high to his neck, skinny jeans, and Converse high tops. The mood slowly diminished when Liam tilted his head away from Taylor, declining a kiss on the lips. Liam managed a tight smile and marched through the flat to the living room, though it was his own.

'I've got you a present,' Taylor said when he returned to the living room, the black matte bag in hand, 'it's nothing special but I hope you like it.'

'Taylor, wait-,' Liam began before he was interrupted.

'It's just a little something to say Merry Christmas and all the best for 2024.'

'I cannot do this anymore with you.'

'What do you mean?'

'I just feel so guilty. All of this sneaking around is not who I am as a person and it's been getting me down so much recently. I feel awful,' Liam admitted.

'Are you serious? I'm not even with him anymore. I've told you that I only want to be with you! I'm serious about that!' Taylor bellowed, the lump in his Adam's apple making it hard to swallow.

'Taylor, seriously, stop it! I don't care whether you're with him or not. The fact is we had sex behind your boyfriend's back which isn't even the worst part. The worst part was telling each other that we loved each other. I'm just as bad in this situation. Do you know how dirty I feel every time that we have sex? Knowing you're going home to... him... who is probably worried sick about you. At first I thought I might have enjoyed it, like it was some sort of sick fantasy. Now I know it's disgusting. Sorry, Taylor. I don't want your gift and I don't want to see you again. All of my friends think I'm the worst person in the world and they tell me I should have got rid of you a long time ago… but there was something about you that made me hold on. This will hurt me to say goodbye… but we need to. Goodbye, Taylor.'

Liam placed a gentle kiss on Taylor's cheek and departed from the flat without a second thought; leaving Taylor clueless and slightly vulnerable, no matter how much his macho persona would disagree. Two of the most important people in his life with such distinct and parallel personas had both departed from his life at the speed of light within 24 hours. He was disposable, just as he treated both of them. For the first time forever, Taylor felt alone. His power had been taken away from him. He sat recounting what Liam had just said, how he felt guilty and dirty when they had sex together, and that his friends thought he was the worst person in the world. *Why do people always get themselves involved in other people's lives?*

In an attempt to reconcile, Taylor picked up the phone and rang Liam for him to return, but he never answered. He rang again. No answer. On the third attempt, Liam answered the call.

'What, Taylor? I have just explained to you that I hold all of this guilt inside of me. It's not fair on me. It's not fair on him, either.'

'Oh my *God*! Stop being so fucking pathetic. What the fuck has it got to do with Callum? I have just told you that he left last night and I have no idea if he's even going to come back. It was his decision to walk out on me so what's happened in the space of a couple of days since the last time we spoke?' Taylor asked.

'Because I should have been spending my Christmas alone with my family, not worrying why somebody with a partner was not texting me back. Bye, Taylor. It was nice knowing you. Please delete my phone number, if you don't mind, please.' And just like that, Liam was gone. Taylor lit a joint and sat thinking of everything that went wrong in less than 24 hours. His boyfriend of ten months had completely left him out of the blue because he couldn't cope with his infidelity any longer, and his second boyfriend couldn't live with knowing that he had a first boyfriend, who was no longer his boyfriend.

Although he enjoyed his own company, he needed someone he could rely on. Somebody submissive, somebody to provide physical support, somebody to have sex with whenever he pleased.

Realising that the two men in his life no longer wanted him, he searched for the App Store on his phone and downloaded the gay dating app *Grindr* in the hopes of finding somebody he could fuck nearby. Taylor kept his profile anonymous; revealing only a name of "**TOP 4 NOW**". He spent over an hour browsing through hundreds of blank pages of young men aged 18-25, increasing his age range by one until he was desperately browsing for men aged 43 and over with no hopes of sex in sight. He sent the same automated copy and paste message to every profile.

Yo. Own place here. Come over and I'll fuck you senseless. Can do anon if needed.

He received repulsive images of ugly penises and gaping holes, time-wasting conversations with no desire to ever meet in person, and people outside of the already stretched allotted age range. Nothing seemed appealing to him regardless of his desperation to unload into someone. After an unsuccessful time on Grindr, he deleted the app, and pleasured himself in bed. He masturbated to a sex tape of him and Callum they had made wired on drugs in late August. He came before the two minute video had finished; toes curled in intense orgasm. He cleaned his mess up with the corner of his bedding and then fell asleep. It was a peculiar feeling to not have someone lay next to him in bed. There was the advantage of room for movement and an extra pillow for his head, the disadvantage being loneliness and no one to fuck.

It was 2024, a new year, and Taylor had still not heard from Callum. His New Year's Eve was spent alone in the flat, binge drinking and sniffing cocaine until early hours in the morning. He blacked out and woke up in a pool of urine on the bathroom floor, blaming the dealer's new supply for his urinary incontinence.

Weeks went by and Callum never returned for his phone. He continued to text and call and got angry when Callum never answered – disregarding the obvious fact that the abandoned phone was still dormant.

He saw Wendy in the street on his way home from work one afternoon and decided to quiz her on Callum's whereabouts. The only people who he thought he would have contacted were Agnes – he had no intention of ever contacting that grotesque lady – or Wendy.

'Hello, Wend. You all right, love?' she was putting cardboard boxes into the brown bin by her garden gate when he approached her, off guard and wary. A tight fake smile signified ongoing resentment. He hated her, and she certainly hated him more. 'How are you?'

'Good, thanks. Where is Callum? I've text him but not had a response.'

'Shit. Well that was what I was going to ask you. He walked out the other night because we had a bit of a barney and I haven't heard from him since. He left his phone in the flat and hasn't come back to pick any of his stuff up. I- ummm… I was debating phoning the police to see if they can file him as a missing person or something like that.'

'What the fuck. Awww, no. You really are a knobhead. My poor little Callum. Your best option is definitely to file a report and see what they say. I'm sure you can report people as soon as they go missing. Not to be nosey, can I ask what you argued about? I know you two have had words in the past, he's been at my door crying… but to actually walk out and leave you? He absolutely adored you so it must have been serious.'

'It's a bit of a long story.'

She invited him in, the fibre optic Christmas tree already dismantled and tinsel discarded on the floor – ready to be boxed and hid in the loft until the next year. They sat at the kitchen table – Wendy was cooking scouse for dinner; the boys were out with her sister – where Taylor opened up about the argument that occurred on Christmas Day – leaving out the infidelity – to which she never responded to except muted tones of disgust through tiny patronising nods of the head. She hated Taylor more than ever because he had ruined a relationship with Callum that made him think the only way he could get away was to disappear without any money, belongings, or goodbyes.

After a short period of silence, 'call the police station or 101,' was all Wendy managed.

'And say what?'

'Tell them that your fucking boyfriend is missing. That's what.' He huffed.

Taylor put the phone firmly to his ear, Wendy unable to hear anything on the other end of the line. 'Hi... I would like to report a missing person. His name is Callum Jones. Yeah, it's the 17th of May 2001. 17 Nightingale Way, Bootle, L30 0BB. Yeah, he's around five-foot six or seven, longish brown hair in a combover fringe, small build, gay.' Wendy was too stunned to speak. The fact he used sexuality as a physical characteristic to describe him, *what a tosser*, she thought to herself.

'What was that? He's not missing. And how would you know that?' Taylor paced around the kitchen like Pac-Man stuck in his maze, the cubed flooring guiding his movement.

'You have a change of address on system? Has he been arrested? *No*? Okay. What the fuck. Where?'

'Temporary accommodation. What is that? A fucking hostel? Is that what it is?' Taylor spoke angrily, 'what fucking hostel? He's my fucking boyfriend, I deserve to know. Fuck confidentiality – I want to know!

Sorry… okay… sorry. Well as long as he is somewhere alive that is all that matters. I'll have a look round tomorrow and see where he could be. Nice one.'

'*Fuck*,' Taylor said when he finished the call – slamming the phone down onto the kitchen table. 'What the hell. They said they've had a change of address registered on the system but wouldn't go any further into it. He could still be missing though, do you think? God, I feel sick. That little fucker. As if he's done this to me.'

'You feel sick? Imagine how he feels. Put yourself in his shoes for one fucking second! Instead of doing nothing but think about yourself. How long has he been there for did they say?'

'They never said. Do you think I should try and find him?'

'He mightn't be able to face the situation which is why he's disappeared off the map. As long as you never physically hurt him, go and find him. Taylor, your relationship wasn't the best. He's a timid lad. You've treated him terribly in the past and he's probably shit scared to come back. Especially if he's been gone for over a week; he probably thinks you wouldn't want him back,' Wendy said.

'I suppose,' Taylor agreed.

They drank their coffee in silence, eventually making conversation about memories they shared with Callum. Drunk nights filled with wine and salted peanuts around Wendy's kitchen table, his plans for the future to run a care agency, previous arguments the two would have that had brought Callum crying to Wendy's door seeking maternal advice. In the end, Wendy had shown solicitude to Taylor for his wrongdoings because he seemed genuinely hurt over Callum's departure. The more he spoke, the more it made him miss the volatility.

He said his goodbyes to Wendy and made his way home. Alone.

The following day, Taylor called in sick for work – at Adrian's request – to spend his day browsing hostels, hoping that he would take him back to where he belonged: their home. Taylor departed the flat at eight in the morning and never returned until seven. 11 hours later: unsuccessful in his quest. He had been to three in the local Sefton area, eight in the city centre, and five located in the south side of Liverpool. Countless arguments with reception staff who couldn't reveal information for confidentiality purposes. Taylor countered that his human rights entitled him to see his partner. Further resistance from staff was the fact he could be an abusive partner and the residents' safety was paramount. The majority of the crowds congregated outside indicated addicts who needed a temporary place to stay, with cracked faces, decayed teeth, frail physiques, and a multitude of bruises covering their arms. He trailed around the flat when he returned home like a lost soul. Movement that lacked emotion except the faint whimpers of exhaustion.

From the first time he had sex with a man, Taylor soon realised men were puppets that lacked free will. Men easier than women, pre-programmed to be overtly sexual. He always felt more satisfied with men because they usually had sex without protection and using a condom was boring.

He once remembered fucking an Albian asylum seeker and contracting gonorrhoea because he was adamant on not using a condom with Enis who had one of the thickest bottoms ever on a man of his small build. It turned out that Enis had entered the UK illegally and was being trafficked for sex by a drug dealer, also from Albania, who was operating a small county lines operation, supplying cocaine and heroin throughout the Merseyside area. Enis' life had been a tragedy.

Taylor was back on *Grindr* and using five other apps for sex. His browsing had become automated, his phone never out his hand whilst he scrolled throughout the evening looking for someone to fuck. In less than a week, Taylor had had unprotected sex with five men, all of the same stature, luckily aged between 18-24, with minimal facial hair, tight skin, and feminine features.

With the first, he made a huge mistake of letting them stay over for the night. After their rowdy sex that never stopped until early hours in the morning – fuelled by alcohol and cocaine – he told the stranger who went by the name of Andrew that he could spend the night.

'Oh, *as if*! Don't be *silly*, this was just sex. I wasn't expecting to stay over, by the way. I hope you don't think that was my intention coming over here,' Andrew said when Taylor offered a room for the night. The sincerity infuriated Taylor because it made him think of Callum, how much he apologised over the slightest inconvenience. However, it made him want Andrew to stay because he thought it would feel like Callum was back in his rightful place.

However, when they both woke simultaneously and he turned over to see a strange face, it infuriated Taylor, who grabbed Andrew and pulled him from bed, forcing him out of the flat. It was clear his intimidation technique had worked because he left just as fast as he ejaculated the night prior.

His approach to sex needed to be different – to be cold, heartless, and aggressive was his new motive. He needed to stop searching for what he once had and learn to fuck people and abandon them as soon as the deed was done. Disposability.

The more that Taylor had sex with strangers, the more it repulsed him. He remained hostile; demanding that they take their clothes off immediately and limiting conversation to single words. He had sex on the sofa with his second encounter from the internet – opting for his hand to be wrapped around the stranger's throat until he came. 'Put your clothes on and leave,' was all that Taylor managed afterwards. *I'm the main character and everybody wants me,* he thought to himself.

Taylor's third victim was forced to get undressed in front of him whilst Taylor pleasured himself. Watching the lad who went by Niall undress like a frightened little boy, shielding his genitals away. He had sex with Niall on the bed and left bruises on his body from strangulation and spanking. Once finished, Taylor told Niall to clean himself in the bathroom whilst he lay scrolling through his phone oblivious to the naked man who wandered around his bedroom, wiping himself down with loose pieces of toilet paper.

His fourth encounter was similar to the previous three. This time he truly felt in control, not just in his behaviour, but also in his brain. They both orgasmed simultaneously; releasing their bodily fluids on one another.

The simplicity of number four made him try with another. They both agreed it would be anonymous and he would come in, be fucked, then leave, never to be seen again. It was perfect until the stranger attempted to kiss him and Taylor forcefully dragged him from the flat. After he left, Taylor lay on his bed and vowed to never engage in sexual relations again, regardless of gender. He was capable of orgasming alone in the same intense way that anyone who gave him head could. The decision had been made that Taylor wanted to be left alone forever.

Time persisted, winter became increasingly colder, with harsh frost and prolonged cold spells. Along with the weather, Taylor's mood deteriorated. He swapped cigarettes to weed and smoked in excess of ten joints a day. He argued with customers in Milton's and roughly handled stock until it broke, even after hours of pedantic sorting. His conduct had not gone unnoticed because Adrian called him to the staffroom one day, his arms – that were engulfed in thick ginger hairs and freckles – crossed in fury.

'Don't you start having a go at me as well, Adrian. I honestly can't deal with all of this at the minute. I've got enough on my plate.'

'You fucking listen to me, Taylor. I am your boss and you do as you're told when you are in work, okay? What the fuck is up with you recently?

You've been like a completely different person recently. What's wrong with you? Is it Callum?'

'Nothing is wrong with me, I'm fine.' Adrian knew he was not fine. The lack of sleep was apparent on his face, he was unable to relax, and his physique lacked the definition it once had.

'Well, you don't seem fine to me. Shouting and swearing at customers who shop here every day of the week. You have potentially lost this place thousands in cash a day. I hate having to be the one to shout at people, but your conduct is shocking. Don't try and deny it because even the way you are now says enough. Stood there with a face like thunder. Plan of action for the rest of the day is for you to go home and don't bother coming back in tomorrow if you are still like this.'

'I don't need to go home, Adrian,' Taylor said quietly.

'I don't care what you think you need. I'm telling you as your boss to go home and have a think about how you're behaving and if you can't change your attitude, don't bother coming back, mate.' He stormed out of the staffroom, slamming the door behind him. An echo rang in his ears.

In consideration of Adrian, he went home and never returned to work for another three days. Sitting in bed for most of the time. Smoking weed and cigarettes, masturbating to gay porn, sniffing cocaine, overthinking, and anxiously waiting for Callum's return. However, one thing that he never did was cry. Tears equalled emasculation.

He wrote notes with poor grammar on his phone to Callum – a tool he had found on the internet that could apparently alleviate anxiety and provide clarity for the mind. Spelling errors. Misplaced punctuation. Abbreviations. Nonsensical wording.

Cal seriously ... I don't even know where to start with this.

I just want to firstly say I'm so sorry for everything that I hav put u through recently. You held on to us for so long to try and make it work and I fucked it up,, I don't know how u done it coz I would've got rid of me a longgg g time ago! But you chose to stay to try and make this work out 4 us and I ruined it like the fcking idiot I am. Am honestly so sorry for everything that I have done to you in the past, all them times I hit you or spoke to you like shit .... callin you names that were just a bunch of lies. U deserved so much better than that. I feel like u deserve to know about the person who the bracelet was for an am sorry for lying abar it.

It wasn't for you an I wasn't goin to ever give 2 you after Xmas ... I lied and I don't know why. His name was Liam an I met him when I went out for a drink once. We ended up havin sex and sort of messaging an I don't even really know what else to say because he has fucked me off as well but all I keep thinking about is you any way. I hope I never hurt u 2 much. You left without an explanation an I honestly thought you woz dead for a while ... I wish I could tell u how sorry I am for what I did ... being away from you has been the hardest thing I've ever had to deal with. You used to irritate me when we woz together but I swear to God I would do anything to have you here now wrecking my head.

My life feels incomplete without you Callum. I hope you still remember me coz I'd love to start this from the start and show you how u deserve to be treated. Like I shud have done from the start when we first met... I knew you was a keeper but I fucked it up and pushed u away and I can't forgive myself. I think if u could forgive me that would be the first step for me to start forgivving myself.

Me an Wendy spoke about u for hours the other day, reminisicing on all the funny times we've had together when we had a drink. She misses you to btw ... she thinks I'm a fool for how I have treated you and I honestly agree with her for once. I still hate her though. I wonder if you come back one day we could all have a drink together and catch up... if you would like to do that?

I know your in a hostel. Is that how much you wanted to get away from me? I couldn't have imagined u to have lasted longer than a day in a fucking hostel! So I'm proud of you for that even if I would have rather you back in our bed with me. But here's hopin that can happen again soon? But yeh I honestly think av learned my lesson and I hope I

see you soon so I can read this out to u an I hope ull give me another chance but I get it if u don't because I don't think ad give me one either.

I honestly am so so so so so so so sorry.

I love you Callum Jones. Forever.

After writing just over 600 words for hours on end – English was never a forte – making minimal tweaks to the body but never the spelling or grammar mistakes, strangely, Taylor did feel calmer. The form of therapy he found in jest was successful, albeit embarrassing.

Although depressed, Taylor had one day of absence left before he would return to work, so he decided that a night out with his cousin Peter was mandatory. It was Thursday which meant happy hour until 11 p.m. throughout the city centre. Free cocaine from Peter, beautiful men and women he could look at from afar, and nightclubs playing dance music.

Within ten minutes, plans were made. Within thirty minutes, Taylor had arrived at The Horses to meet his cousin Peter and his acquaintance "Big Alan" who lived up to the nickname; with a gargantuan stomach that hung over his jeans, likely from beer, lack of exercise, and an unhealthy diet. Peter looked different since the last time Taylor had seen him. They looked similar around the eyes and nose – like cousins could – but his grey hairs had multiplied, he had gained a little weight, his wrinkles had deepened, and he looked exhausted around the eyes. 'Do not have children. Ever. They drain the soul out of you, I'm telling you,' Peter asserted over his pint of beer.

Taylor loved his older cousin because he made all of his problems feel miniscule, like there was nothing treacherous in the world because the only time that humans needed to focus on was the present. Peter reassured Taylor that there would be another man – or woman – out there – he sometimes forgot that he was bisexual – or that maybe Callum would return in the future.

One drink turned to two, two to five, and before they knew it, The Horses was closing early and they wanted to continue the night to enjoy themselves and the familiar presence of family like adolescent times. They headed to Heaven in the city centre because they knew it was open until late. Peter and Alan collectively thought that Taylor needed male attention, though against his own will. He assured them he had had enough sex to last a lifetime, them arguing against his hesitation.

'Stop being so boring. It won't do you any harm,' Peter mumbled in the back of the taxi on their way to the city centre.

When they ran out of cocaine from inhaling the remains in the cab, Taylor left Peter at the bar whilst he headed for the toilets to find another dealer, agitated to spend his own money – or debt – instead of relying on Peter's supply for the evening. He found a scally who gave him a deal of three for £50 on cocaine, which put him back in an overdraft, due less pay because of his recurrent absence. Thus far, the crisp feeling of its purity made it worthwhile, the intoxication imminent. He sat for a couple of minutes alone with his head rested on the door of the cubicle, an internal pep talk to return to work for his own sanity. After enough cocaine to last half an hour, he journeyed back to the bar to find Peter and Alan. He felt the skin of his warm arms rub against numerous queer men as he exited the cubicle; looks of admiration from young passers-by.

His heart stopped beating when he saw who stood before him. A sight he never thought he would see again, especially with throw-up pouring from its mouth.

It was him.

The End is Near

CHAPTER SEVEN

Looking at one another was a coexistence of pleasure and past trauma. Glee mixed with apprehension. Life and death. As they stared at each other unsure how to proceed, Callum's eyes seemed petrified, like a deer in headlights. The expulsion of alcohol dripped down from the exterior of his lips to the floor and down the stairs, as if forming a path from one soul to the other. Neither of them knew how to react in the situation. *The amount of time we've spent together and I don't even know how to communicate with him,* Taylor thought to himself. In spite of being fuelled on cocaine and alcohol, the note on his mobile was burning a hole in the back of his jeans pocket. Callum was clueless, mysterious, pale, and frail. The lack of sunshine in Heaven made his skin glisten in the overhead fluorescent lighting that lit the walkway to the toilets; the rest of the club dark except for colourful disco lights behind.

Taylor took a slow step forward, as though approaching a delicate mammal in conservation, which Callum reciprocated in slow strides forward, until as proximate as could be.

The End is Near

'Jesus Christ, Callum. Where the fuck've you been? I've been looking for you everywhere. I've been worried sick about you. You left without your phone. How are you?' Taylor attempted to remain calm but struggled to forget how Callum had willingly abandoned their home with no explanation and had him assuming he had been abducted or murdered on a street corner by one of them seedy streetwalking serial killers you saw on documentaries. However, the anger quickly evaporated when he realised his love for him; two lost souls who had finally been reunited by an act only the universe could have consummated.

'Them trainers... I... I bought you them for Christmas,' Callum said in an angsty tone. For a few seconds, he just stood and stared at Taylor's shoes. Strangers by nature.

'Well, it was nice seeing you, Taylor. Look after yourself,' Callum said, disappearing back into the crowd of queer men, women, heterosexuals, strangers, lovers. Rushing through the crowd, Taylor chased him, grabbing him by the hand before he had the opportunity to leave once again.

'Callum, please. Can I talk to you somewhere more private? I know you probably hate me but it's important,' Taylor pleaded into Callum's ear, feeling the heat of his cheek. 'Please, Callum. I've fucked up and I'm not expecting anything from this but I have things I need to say to you.'

Looking at Taylor's lips, kissing him was the only thing that Callum wanted to do.

'No!' Callum shouted, releasing himself from his grip and slipping further away into the crowd of dancers.

'Callum! Please. I am *begging* you now.'

'I have nothing to say to you,' Callum said, his lips pressed against his earlobe.

'Please. I promise it won't be a long conversation. Please, Callum,' he tried again.

'Fine. Let me tell my friends because I've been gone for a while. I'll meet you outside in two minutes.'

Callum headed across the dancefloor to Ian and Kate who danced amusingly to a house-infused Madonna rendition, surrounded by pleasure seekers of all different shapes and sizes, dancing different moves and twirls rhythmically. He told Ian that he was catching up with a friend outside and would be back within ten minutes. Ten daunting minutes with Taylor before normality.

The End is Near

The icy temperature took Callum's breath away as he climbed up the staircase from Heaven to the forgotten outside world. It was late but people were still queueing up to enter. Cigarettes passed around like secrets. The rain was heavy. The wind howled. The city centre road was eery, the bright bricked Georgian buildings contrasted with the darkness of the sky. The pavements were illuminated by desolate street lamps as women strode past with their bare legs revealed, drunken men chanting gross comments sexualising the innocent. The disordered night was other-worldly. Faded beats and whispers of laughter emanated from inside of the club; the air thick with cigarette smoke, beer, and exhaust fumes. Above, the city hummed, carrying with it the light buzz of traffic and the wail of police sirens.

Taylor was waiting to the left of the club, a cigarette hanging from his mouth soaked by rain. The sight of him made butterflies fly inside of Callum's stomach and not in an endearing way. He felt anxious being so proximate to his abuser. Callum paced passed him down an alleyway to the side of the club. Taylor followed suit. It stunk of beer, bins, and urine, like every side street.

'Right, so what do you have to say to me, Taylor?' Callum asked, lighting a cigarette.

'I'm sorry. So sorry, Callum. I have j-just… missed you *sooo* much,' he lit a cigarette also.

Callum sniggered to himself. The only time Taylor seemed to express his emotions was intoxicated. How pathetic he felt to be giving him the time of day when he had chosen to disrespect what they shared together. He needed to be strong. His new life as a single man, the valuable friendship with Ian, new job, promotion, and financial independence fluttered before his eyes like a ghostly spirit. The tables had turned. Somebody who had taken away his innocence many times – a thought flickered, Taylor raping him until he lay crying for hours, questioning what he had done wrong to deserve that level of disrespect – was now stuttering to get his words out. Seeing him vulnerable was unexpected, especially after so long apart because Callum thought he would've forgotten about him and moved on with whoever he had been shagging behind his back.

'Is that it? Come on, Taylor. My friends are waiting inside for me,' Callum prompted impatiently. 'You're honestly a joke. You know what, I honestly don't care what else you have to say. It was a bad idea me coming out here. I do appreciate the sentiment but this is finished between me and you. I have nothing else to say. Goodbye, Taylor. Take care of yourself,' he took a long drag of his cigarette until it burned the back of his throat.

'Wait! Sorry. Please just listen. I've written you a note on my phone that I wanted to say to you… if I ever saw you again. I know, cringey bastard, aren't I? I found it on the internet, felt like an absolute beast writing it but hey ho. Want to hear it?'

'Whatever,' Callum said.

Taylor grabbed his phone from his pocket and started reciting it like a priest reading the sacrament, stumbling on the many grammatical errors, making Callum chuckle sympathetically. Callum felt a mixture of emotions at Taylor's sermon. Happiness. Sadness. Anger. Guilt. Anxiety. Internally, he had forgiven Taylor because enough time had elapsed to not carry hatred in his heart. It didn't take long after moving into HHI to realise that trauma in his adult years would fuse with his childhood, always carried around like a sentimental keepsake. However, Callum also doubted that he would ever be able to forget. His future relationships would be constructed on the suffering caused. Sexual assault would be expected with affection. Physical violence would be expected with loving touch. When it concluded with the words read that he loved him forever, he burst into tears for reasons unknown.

'I'm sorry if I've upset you,' Taylor said, showing a sympathetic smile with nicotine stained teeth.

'I don't know why I'm crying,' he was confused by his sudden change of mood.

'It must be because I'm such a good writer, right?'

'Ha. You're *so* funny. But let's not forget all of the times that you hurt me. Do you think I'm ever going to forget all of that? The times you raped me, or spoke to me like I was a piece of shit, or hit me, or ignored me for hours whilst you were out, obviously fucking God knows who, whilst I sat in bed worried to death thinking you would never come back. I stayed with you because I didn't know any different. I loved you. I still love you. I think a part of me will always love you forever. Our relationship is grained in my mind because in one instance, you showed me love, the other you showed me what love certainly isn't meant to be. You were never ready for a relationship the way I was. You wanted someone to be available for sex at the drop of a hat. You saw me as an object you could fuck whenever you wanted. And I mean, whenever you wanted. When I was trying to sleep, when I was sad, when I said "no, I don't want to do this tonight, please". I don't think I will ever be romantic with somebody else again and I have you to thank for my many trust issues. I still haven't spoken to my nan. That woman gave me everything she had so I could have the best possible life and I gave all of it away. For what? For a relationship that was reminiscent of everything I was trying to escape.'

They broke down simultaneously and it was like the world drew them together in a warm embrace. They hugged one another in the darkness of the alleyway, cigarettes still lit. Anyone who walked past and saw the duo wouldn't have seen it for what it was: love; forgiveness; trauma. They would have simply saw two drunken idiots crying about something unrelated, like how much they enjoyed high school together, or how handsome the other was.

'I'm honestly so sorry, Cal. I am so fucking sorry for what I have done.'

'I know. I know you are. What's done is done. I forgive you but it will never be the way it was before.' The words acted as the final chapter in their novella together. The finale to the script. The credits of their movie.

'Cal, can we please try this again? I promise I'll love you. I'll be there for you, I'll protect you, I'll be the best boyfriend ever,' Taylor pleaded.

'I'm sorry, Taylor. I just can't do it to myself. Bye, again. I appreciate your cute little message. It was beautiful. Times have changed and I'm trying to be a different person now. Goodbye.' The therapy sessions with Ed had paid off because his outlook on the situation had shifted in ways that he never thought possible. He now realised his worth – regardless of his emotional response to the note, though expected when somebody declares their undying love for you – and that only he could give himself everything deserved. He never needed a toxic relationship with occasional bouts of happiness. All Callum needed for survival was himself.

Callum left without another word, jolting down the stairs into Heaven before he could be stopped, again. The area where they previously stood was filled with strangers. They weren't at the bar either. He searched the toilets but there were no signs of Ian anywhere. His eyes became hazy and the quiet outside made the club overstimulating upon his return. It reeked of sweat, dirt, poppers, and beer.

Cal wer the fuck have u gone?

We're going home !! We're in work tomoro - phone me when you get this

Phone me

DO u wnat a pizza delivering to the hospital

I mean hostel.

When Ian never responded to his phone calls, he realised that he had been gone for over half an hour; time moving so fast they likely never anticipated his return. Being alone in the club was not how Callum wanted to spend the rest of his night. He felt lonely and more drinking would further increase the risk of a gruesome hangover tomorrow. In light of this, Callum concluded that he needed fresh air to acknowledge everything that had happened. Deciding to take the walking route home through the cold darkness of the winter with no one, except himself and his thoughts.

He lit a cigarette once he got out of Heaven and took a right, making his way past the flocks of drunken revellers high on alcohol and ecstasy. Considering Ed's encouraging words, Callum contemplated his encounter, and knew that he would for weeks, or even months. He needed to overanalyse the situation. Callum was happily single, likely remaining single for an eternity. As he wandered through the city centre – it always seemed more creepy of a night – the floor was wet and puddles of rainwater had soaked through his pants. Closed pubs, crowds waiting for taxis, and congregations of homeless people on every corner. Inhaling a large drag of his cigarette whilst looking over his shoulder in fear of a homeless man shouting slurs he couldn't decipher, Callum knocked full force into a large figure walking in the opposite direction.

'Hey, watch where you're fucking walk-... Cal... oh, sorry... I never realised that was you,' the familiar voice said. A ghost of his past reincarnated for the second time that night.

'Sorry. I didn't know it was you.' Taylor apologised again. 'Where are you walking to? Do you want me to walk with you or drop you off in a taxi? Our Peter left me because I was gone for so long,' Taylor said.

'I was left too, by my friends. No, I'll be okay. I want the fresh air and to be alone for a while. Thanks anyways. Bye again, for the hundredth time tonight,' Callum managed a small laugh.

As he continued on the cold expedition through the city centre back to his hostel, footsteps followed him, the splash of heavy feet strolling through puddles. He turned around and Taylor was still following him; their eyes meeting sharply once again. 'I'm fine, Taylor. I'm only round the corner, please. I just want to be left alone for my walk.'

'Well, can I walk behind you? I just want to make sure you get home okay. I won't knock for you to play out, don't worry. How is life in the hostel? Wow, you in a hostel… I would pay good money to see that. I shouldn't joke about it when I'm the reason you are there. Sorry, I was just trying to make the mood less sour.'

'The mood isn't sour. I'm walking home and you're basically following me. I'm big enough to walk on my own, Taylor.' He continued to walk as Taylor continued following, eventually giving up and allowing him to trail behind. Callum shouted over his shoulder whilst he spoke, Taylor remaining his allocated five steps behind. He spoke about life since he left – from finding emergency accommodation at the hostel and the vulnerable people there, ongoing therapy sessions with Ed, leaving Mike's to find another career, and his promotion to store manager.

'I'm so proud of you, Cal. You deserve the world and more.'

The journey back to the hostel was filled with talks about their contrasting lives: one aspiring for a better future, the other dwelling on the past.

'It's been nice seeing you again, Cal. I hope you can forgive me for what I've done to you. I truly see how much of a cunt I was to you now and I'm honestly so sorry,' Taylor said before he continued on, 'before you go… I didn't say all I wanted to say before. I don't think you honestly understand how sorry I am. I love you so much and I wish we could just try this all over again. I miss you more than anything in the world. I've never truly felt love or what it felt like to be loved until I met you and I've fucked it up.'

'Taylor, seriously, *stop*. I want to go to bed!' he shouted.

'*No*! Callum! I don't think you actually understand, so please just let me finish or I'll never forgive myself. I should've treated you the way you deserve to be treated and I can now. Why I ever laid eyes on anyone else when I had you in front of me is beyond me. I've been off work because my moods have become so erratic I've been flipping out on everyone. I was legged by that fella I bought the bracelet for because he didn't want to be with me because I had a fella. That made me realise that all I wanted was you. I've had sex with a few people thinking it would fill a void and it did the complete opposite, it just made me want you even more than before. I don't really go out anymore, except tonight, obviously. I have changed and I want to treat you how you should be treated. Please just come and see me one night this week; not even for sex. Just so we can have a proper catch up and you can get your stuff.'

'Taylor, what can you not seem to grasp about the concept of no? I don't want to cuddle you.'

'You need to come and get your stuff from the flat. So why not come and get the stuff and then that will be it?'

'I've already replaced most of the things I left over at our-... your flat,' he quickly corrected the phrase. Taylor felt a pang of sadness at the realisation that their home was only his now.

'I've kept it all. There is quite a lot of stuff so I don't think it would fit all in one run in a taxi.'

'Fine. But I swear to God – no sex, no cuddling. I'll come and get all of my stuff. Ed will be fuming I'm even thinking of doing this but getting my stuff back is okay. Don't expect anything out of this and please take this for what it is… it's me doing you a favour. Not because I want to… because I think you deserve it. The tables have turned and even after the things you've done, it's not nice to think of you being upset. Now I'm seriously going to bed, goodnight.'

They exchanged numbers since Callum had changed his, excited to fall asleep on his thin prison-like mattress, with an alarm set to wake in four hours' time. His mind raced for the duration; tossing and turning; examining everything that happened; surveying his ex's words. It would've been easier if he faced the demon he once knew but Taylor had manipulated into something much worse: a vulnerable organism.

Was so nice to see you Callum. You look well

Hope u got home safe

I need ya and I miss ya xxX

U awake yet?

He text back, irritated at the familiarity.

Stop texting me please. I will come to yours later tonight. I will text you when I am outside later.

A gruelling shift at work was made up of sorting bulk deliveries of a new cheap collaboration between an influencer and Primark which consisted of a range of soft cotton pyjamas, slippers, stationery, and homeware. As he managed the store and its operations, Callum struggled to think of anything except the night before, paired with a terrible headache from all of the wine consumed.

When he got back to the hostel late that evening, Ian was at the reception with a cup of tea waiting for his return – like clockwork. Ian later confessed that he booked leave for that day and only visited the hostel to check in on his hangover, which Callum thought was quite strange and sad. He could never imagine himself going to work to check in on someone, even if they were the nicest person to grace planet Earth.

'Where the fuck did you go last night? One minute you were there, the next you disappeared and never came back. Sorry we left you, Kate started vomiting and it was time to take her home. Didn't help going home any earlier because I'm still destroyed today. The older you get, the worse these hangovers get. Make the most of your outings now.'

'I saw an old friend so we had a little catch up outside. I thought it would only be ten minutes but he wanted to fill me in on his life. His mum isn't well so he got a bit upset,' Callum lied, feeling instant guilt for being deceitful about such a sensitive topic.

'Oh, wow. That's sad. What's wrong with her?'

'Stage three breast cancer. She's a lovely woman. Used to spend so much time in hers as a kid. Going to the hospital with him soon to see her,' Callum lied again.

'Well that's nice, I'll drop you off if you want?' Ian offered.

'No, *no*! I'm going to meet him and get the bus together.'

'I'll pick him up too, then?'

'Honestly, Ian. Don't worry. You're hungover, go home away from this shithole and get your head down. You deserve a proper day off. It's the weekend, I hope to not see you again until Monday.'

'You know what, you're right. I do deserve some rest. I think I'll watch a film when I get home – a classic maybe. Tarantino? No. Hitchcock. Rear Window; Psycho; North by Northwest. What do you think?'

'No idea.'

'Okay, Rear Window it is.' They spoke for a while and planned to go for another quiz night at the end of March. 'Kate will definitely have recovered by then,' Ian promised.

Arriving just after eight o'clock Friday evening at the flat he used to call home was anxiety inducing. The entirety of the journey was filled with past memories – cooking together; war documentaries they watched on the sofa; sex they had when his body was draped in cheap lingerie at Taylor's request. A period of his life that he once thought as the epitome of happiness was nothing but depression now. He smoked two cigarettes on his walk from the bus stop to the flat, anxiously pacing the streets of the suburban area. The same lack of greenery; street cats hidden under cars; chipped paint on houses; yobs on street corners; cigarette butts and chewing gum aging the pavements.

The buzz of the foyer door had been fixed since the last time there. Numerous residents of the block – including Taylor – had complained to the housing of a problem with the door. It buzzed for hours after somebody had called, and it never locked once opened. For a nanosecond, all he thought about was the door, until the cold touch of the handle jolted him back to his daunting reality. It seemed bizarre for Callum to visit this place as a stranger: his past home now a stranger's abode.

Taylor opened the door before he knocked, eyeing his arrival from the flat window, making Callum wonder if he saw him pacing back and forth down the street smoking a cigarette. The wide smile and gleaming eyes made him feel anxious, like he was expecting something other than the chore of retrieving his personal items.

'Hi, Taylor,' he said, gliding past him, through to the living room, throwing himself on the reassuring leather of the sofa. The flat was untouched. No further decorating had been done, the second-hand sofa still screamed underneath your weight, the kitchen still had its wooden cupboards and faux granite worktops, and cheap prints of flowers still hung from the walls. Callum noticed the sharp stench of bleach throughout the house, sniggering at the thought of Taylor cleaning before his arrival.

'Nice to see you again, Cal.'

'You look rough.'

'You don't look too good yourself.'

'Okay,' was all Callum managed.

Taylor huffed and removed himself from the living room, slamming the door, before returning back in ten seconds carrying something in his hand. Callum noticed it was the same matte packaging as the reason why they were no longer living under the same roof.

'Taylor, no. Don't start trying to play mind games with me. Seriously, I'm in a good place and I do not need your pity presents.'

'Please, just take it. Or at least open it, I know you will like it.'

Callum opened the giftbox to see a gold necklace with **"NAN"** engraved on a feather shaped locket at the centre of the necklace. The tears began to stream out of his eyes in a heavy current; removing any residue hatred from his heart. The necklace shook in the palm of his shaky hands, tears dampening the gold.

The End is Near

Callum never knew how to respond to the offering. He was appreciative of the necklace and its sentimental value but the situation between them was still sour and he knew not to show more vulnerability. Graciousness was something that his grandmother had taught him; to always be courteous in situations when others couldn't be.

'You should never have done this. I-I don't know what to say… thank you, Taylor, I guess,' he hugged him tightly but immediately regretted his action as too friendly. 'Sorry, I shouldn't have hugged you like that. I don't want you to think I've forgotten about everything. But honestly, thank you from the bottom of my heart. This is a gorgeous necklace and it's ten times better than the bracelet you bought for that other person… but I didn't want you to get me this. I told you I forgive you, but I just come here to get my stuff. So I cannot possibly accept this, Taylor. Return it and get your money back.'

'I can't get my money back because it's personalised. Just take it and pawn it for some money if you would like.'

'It seems such a waste.'

'Then wear it.'

'I think I will.'

'I can't do this any longer,' Taylor whispered. With all of his strength – not much was needed for Callum's thinness – he pulled him close to his body, their breath heavy and warm on one another. The first real reunion kiss was intimate, like the universe had been longing for them to reunite. Neither could stop, they craved each other. Taylor wanted to feel him under his skin, travelling through his nervous system to the core of the world: his heart. The relationship was to be rebirthed in a way unimaginable – one of pure pleasure with satisfaction of every need. He pulled Callum's top off and then his own.

'I don't know if I'm strong enough for this. You hurt me badly,' Callum muttered.

'Trust me.' Strangely, Callum did trust him. Taylor pulled his pyjama shorts down, feeling it graze against the interior of Callum's thigh. 'I've missed your body so much. You are so beautiful.'

Wrapping his hands around Callum to ensure his fingers were locked tightly, Taylor scooped him up in his arms and carried him to the bedroom. He placed Callum on the bed like he was a delicate object – something that needed nurturing and protecting. They continued kissing intimately; both of their lips caressing each other whilst their tongues slid around one another's mouths. Callum's petite figure slot perfectly into Taylor's large build, like the last piece of a jigsaw puzzle.

'I can't wait to feel you inside of me. It's been so long.'

'I've missed you so much, baby boy. Please never leave me again.' Callum lowered his head down Taylor's body; tenderly kissing and sucking the skin on his neck. It felt different this time, Callum thought, because he wasn't being forced. He was free to do as he pleased with his intimate areas. Once the moaning started and he was close to climax, Callum squatted on it, feeling him inside an area that had not been touched since him.

'That was amazing. Hands down the best sex I've ever had,' Taylor said, a large smile spread across his face, 'what are we doing now? Are we getting back together?' he asked.

'No.'

'You answered that too quickly for my liking.'

'Sorry, but I don't think we should ever get back together. Coming to see you tonight... I had no intention of having sex with you but here we are. It was nice, I won't lie to you. I don't want to think that everything is going to be okay. No matter how passionate the sex is... it doesn't erase the past and what you did to me. You cheated on me multiple times, I know you did, and I allowed it. You sexually assaulted me at least three times a week. You gaslighted me, thinking I was the worst boyfriend in the world, so no, I don't think we should get back together.'

'I get that, sorry for asking. Let's take it slow then. You and me, pal. Nobody else.'

Callum felt nauseous at the words rolling off of Taylor's tongue, when he had made a vow to himself that it would only be himself in the equation.

Anxiety. Anxiety. Anxiety. Yet, the only thing that had calmed his mind was the gentle touch of his palm against his.

They spent the night together, naked, with Callum entangled in Taylor's broad arms until the morning. They managed to have sex for one more time which Callum thought would be their final.

'I'm going to miss you so much,' Taylor said – just after eight a.m. They spent the night together.

'Mhm.'

'Seriously, I am. Don't you believe me?'

'I do believe you – I just don't want you to miss me. This was sex, Taylor. That's all. A hungover mistake,' he said brutally.

'Wow.'

'It's the truth,' Callum responded, putting yesterday's disgraced outfit back on, 'I have to go now. Goodbye. Thank you again for my gift.' He gave him a gentle kiss on the lips and left for the hostel, rapidly dressing for another day at work: four hours extra money in his pocket.

Only when his shift had finished did Callum realise that he forgot the reason he went in the first place: for his lost belongings. No matter how stupid he felt, he felt content about the night they shared together. It felt like a night of normalcy.

Six texts Callum had received from Taylor: it was moving too fast. Soon enough, sex would turn into cuddles, then dates, then another relationship, then heartbreak, and then regret.

Miss u already x

Hope u have a boss day in work kid xx

Can't stop thinkin about you… are we seeing eachother later definitely? You never got your stuff! X

Hope your ok. I'm hard at the thought of you next to me in bed x

???

Sorry I know we need to take this slow. Hope ya day is going well xx

When he returned to his interim home, Ian invited him for drinks with another friend called Becky in a pub around the corner from the hostel. The Berliner. Located down a seedy alleyway in the city centre, the boozer was an oblong shaped building with brutalist architecture, bare concrete walls and large wooden tables with benches, that DJ played techno beats mashed with indie songs, and it had a rep for being somewhat of an LGBT safe space. No pub quizzes and only German beers, spirits, and wine were sold. He politely declined the invitation.

'I've got plans sorry,' Callum told him.

'You? Plans? With whom?' Ian grinned.

'Just a friend. You know the one I saw the other night in Heaven?'

'Oh. You mean your ex? Come on, Callum. Don't try and kid me. You can't kid a kidder. Lying about his mum having cancer, tut-tut. This scatty place is rubbing off on you. I never had you out to be a compulsive liar, especially about something so bad. That lad is the reason you're living in this dump. Please don't go there again. Imagine what Ed would have to say!' Ian said.

'Callum, all of this hard work we have put in to get you back to a place of happiness, it seems to me as though you are throwing it all away for instant gratification. You need to imagine where you see yourself in five years' time. Do some homework and imagine what you would want for your 30-year-old self,' Ian said mockingly, imitating Ed's husky, masculine voice.

'I never lied! As if. It isn't my ex-boyfriend.'

'Callum?'

'Okay, fine! I'm so sorry for lying. I've never lied about anything like that before, God forbid anything happens to me now as a form of karma. Okay, so we spoke… I'm going to pick up some of my stuff later. Oh, Ian, don't look at me like that!' It was a look of "what are you doing?" mixed with "you silly, silly boy".

'I promise, I've got control of the situation now. We won't ever get back together. I'm going to get my stuff, have a cup of tea, and then leave. He's been cheating on me, he could be riddled with anything,' he said, thinking of the potentials of an STI from the night before.

'Just a word of advice… I've ran back to exes in the past and at the time it seemed like the best thing to do. I was just being fucking stupid. Luckily, my relationship now is amazing and I've never experienced love like it. He's my biggest supporter. What you had, I know you know anyway, but that wasn't love. Or quite frankly, you wouldn't be living in this shithole of a hostel. Be careful, and you know where I am if you need anything, always.'

Whilst Callum appreciated the concern from Ian, his patronising talk of how amazing his relationship was irked him. Callum knew his situation was an abuse of power. He vowed to himself that he would not have sex again: with the man who sexually abused him regularly.

After a quick shower – in the clinical white shared bathroom, full of damp towels, dirty tiles, and grubby flooring – and a change of clothes, Callum got the bus to Taylor's, arriving just after six o'clock when the sky was dark and the strong winds catapulted the brown leaves through the streets. They greeted at the door in an awkward manner, Callum opting for a handshake whilst Taylor drew him close for a hug.

'Follow me,' Taylor led him straight into the bedroom and began to take off his fresh clothing until he was in nothing but underwear and socks.

'I can't do this.'

'Yes, you can. We did this yesterday and you seemed to enjoy it.'

As Callum pleaded his doubts, Taylor continued to explore the chill of his body; stroking his hair gently, rubbing the tip of his nose that was red from the wind outside, massaging his stomach with his knuckles.

'I really can't do this, Taylor. I don't want you to get the wrong impression.'

'Please, baby. I'll be gentle.'

'I thought we were taking this slow.'

'We are, but I want you now.'

'Take me then,' with his command, they had passionate sex just like the night before, with Callum on top of Taylor.

Callum spent the following six evenings – unwisely – in the same rigid routine of finishing work and then descending to Taylor's bed where they would have sex, cuddle, watch movies, sleep, and then separate for the day to attend work, and then repeat. Work. Sex. Repeat. Although it was refreshing to hang around with a completely different version of the man he once loved more than anything in the world, the mundanity of their routine was becoming too intense. His regime had become standardised; nothing else given the opportunity.

He planned a solo date to the cinema to watch a new horror movie but by the time he got round to it, the next sequence of movies had taken its place. He had grown fond of the spontaneity that living on his own – although with 30 others – had given him. The ability to finish work and be alone, working overtime to buy himself new clothes, completing chores in his claustrophobic bedroom, exploring new hobbies like crocheting, or spending time with Ian. The capacity to walk for miles down the Albert Dock with no thoughts except the pitter-patter of his shoes against the pavement; different music emanating from passing cars, Shakira to Bruce Springsteen.

The looming regret of too much time spent together caused anxiety for him, so he spent the following week away from Taylor as a trivial form of independent civilisation.

'You are the main character in your life, Callum. Goals. Mistakes. Feelings. Don't be concerned with anybody except yourself. It is only you who can decide how it all pans out for the narrator. However, sexual trauma so brutal as what we have previously discussed may not be the route that your life should be going down again, even if it is your own decision. If you feel strong enough to give it another chance, then amazing. Go for it. However, I would hate it to ruin everything that you have built for yourself in the past couple of months, no matter how turbulent it has been,' Ed said in their next therapy session together. They were nine sessions in. Their final date unknown.

'I thought being away from him for a couple of months would make me forget about him. It failed. I just don't want to be hurt again. I don't know what I want, to be honest with you, Ed.'

The End is Near

'Unfortunately, I won't be able to tell you what to do. I can give advice based on what you have told me in previous sessions and then make somewhat of a reasoned decision, but regrettably, I can't tell you what to do. I will help you along the way no matter what. You are a lot stronger than what you think. I do feel as though you are believing in yourself a bit more – would you say that's an accurate statement, Callum?'

'I suppose so. I do feel more confident in myself and the decisions I make. I know I don't need him because I've survived this long without him. Do you think that he will hurt me again, Ed?'

'I don't know. I have never met him nor will I ever. You only tell me snippets during our sessions.'

'Would you go back to him if you were me?'

'Callum, I can't answer that question. Only you can. Look, our session is coming to an end now – why don't you do some thinking over the weekend. List all the pros and cons of giving him another chance. Stop being so hard on yourself, you have loads of time to decide what you want to do.'

The session ceased and he felt more confused than before.

Three evenings after his last session with Ed, when he lay draped over his structured body, their feet entangled, Taylor stroking his back, he whispered passionately in his ear. 'I have something to tell you.'

'What?' Callum asked, feeling Taylor's heartbeat pumping against his ear.

'I love you so much,' Taylor muttered. 'Did you hear what I said?' he asked when Callum didn't respond.

'Yes. I'm so tired today, I think I might try and fall asleep. Goodnight,' Callum replied.

'Do you love me too?'

'You should know how I feel without me having to tell you.'

'What does that mean?'

'You don't have to say "I love you" every second of the day to be in love, is what I mean. Goodnight now, I'm tired.' He fell asleep within five minutes.

The exchange made Callum withdraw. They shared a bed together for over a year, they halved their bills, they knew each other's deepest secrets, but that was the past. Callum had seemingly allowed him back in. Acknowledging it scared him. Kissing, hugging, having sex. *Love, love, love.*

Two nights apart ascertained they could survive alone, with Taylor struggling more than Callum. Callum spent his time at work, alone wandering around the city centre until late, or with Ian at a drive-through cinema they had found on the outskirts of Liverpool. Taylor got stoned in bed on his days off work and watched aggressive heterosexual porn.

The next romantic encounter between Taylor and Callum was a planned trip to a casual food chain that specialised in chicken. Burgers, thighs, pittas, wraps. What Taylor had assumed would be a cheap night resulted in shock horror when the bill came to £47 for two chicken burgers with sides. They then watched a new horror movie out in the cinema called *Don't Sit Still* that Callum rated a seven out of ten. The rating was based on a gothic atmosphere which he liked, complimenting the cinematography and acting, but criticism was directed at the abrupt ending. Whilst out, Taylor bought him a cheap bouquet of flowers. They spent the night together spooning; delicately entangled. The next morning when he arose and there was no Taylor, anxiety made his chest tighten.

'Taylor. Are you in here?' Callum shouted through the flat with a croaky morning voice. No response. Three more attempts of recall until he climbed out of bed, put on sliders to avoid his feet having to touch the matted carpet, and stumbled through the abode, following the faint noises exuding from the kitchen. In there, Taylor was stood naked, making breakfast for the pair. The different scents revealed that eggs, bacon, and toast were on the menu.

'Good morning, Cal. Breakfast is on the way. Did you see the living room or did your puffy eyes stop you?'

Callum turned around to see "**GOOD LUCK**" standing high on eight silver coloured balloons. He walked over to observe the balloons up close, opening a blue envelope on the floor.

To Callum,

Good luck in your new job as the store manager of Primark! No one deserves it more. So proud of you and everything you have achieved.

Hope you have a good day in work.

P.S. when you read this, ask me to ask you a question.

Lots of love, Taylor xxXxx

'Thank you. Thank you… so much. You didn't have to do any of this, Taylor,' Callum said.

'You deserve it, I'm proud of you,' Taylor replied over the crackling of the eggs on the frying pan.

'Ask me a question.'

Callum's heart sunk inside because he knew what would be asked. He felt obliged to say yes, even with doubts. However, Taylor had never been this thoughtful before. It now felt like real love.

'Will you be my boyfriend, Callum Jones?'

And there it was.

'Y-yes. I would love to. I love you.'

A passionate kiss entwined in Taylor's muscly arms felt like a warm summer holiday in the Balearics. Their tongues entangled in a deep-rooted desire for each other felt like air conditioning in 40 degree Celsius heat.

The motivation to grow in all aspects raged inside of him. He wanted a happy relationship, a steady job, a support system of friends, a healthy mind, no drugs, and to drink controlled levels of alcohol.

He spent eight hours in Primark that day, completing mundane e-learning modules for his new title as the store manager. Teaching him the logistics of management, health and safety, leadership skills, how to deliver profits, modern day slavery, and the values of Primark.

No matter how boring this could seem to the average person, life was perfect, Callum thought to himself. He was flourishing.

CHAPTER EIGHT

'Taylor! Where the hell are we going? I've had my eyes closed for about ten minutes and I would really appreciate if I could actually see where I was going,' Callum said.

'Just a little longer. I will guide you,' Taylor said.

Taylor held his large hands over Callum's eyes – the bitter stench of stale cigarettes on his fingertips eroding Callum's senses – to avoid him seeing anything except darkness. His hands hunched over his face meant Callum was concealed away from the world with nothing in sight, making him feel slightly anxious, out of control, and confused. What if he got hit by a car? What if somebody ran at him with a knife? Would he be able to trust Taylor to ensure that he avoided danger and survived? A relationship without trust was doomed to end tragically.

They continued on by foot. The textures alternating under the grip of their trainers: thick concrete to crisp branches; wet mud to hard gravel; the grizzly texture of sand making its way into the corners of their shoes.

The End is Near

Callum loathed sand – the smell of it, the texture, and how you found grains buried inside unspeakable places after a visit to the beach. The further they walked, the thicker it got, feeling it graze against his ankles through his socks. He could hear the sound of water; the tide approaching the shore and the cold April air when the sun set later than usual and there was hope of some form of summer.

'You can open your eyes now,' Taylor said.

Callum opened his eyes to what he expected; one of the local beach coasts. A major advantage of Liverpool was accessibility to the coast, fresh saltwater, and watching the sun set under the straight blue line of the water.

The sky was violently pink in colour – a vivid fuchsia background painted with dusty pink clouds floating past. The sight was beautiful, his favourite colour of the sky interweaved with blue opaque waves that stretched as far as the eye could see, Earth's circular curve allowing for no ending in sight. The observation of Mother Nature's creation made his heart warm, a large smile unable to be removed. Experiencing nature with his soulmate was one of life's greatest treasures. Their relationship had grew stronger, their mindfulness for one another's needs strengthening their bond, and the capacity to live somewhat separate lives with their own social lives made it less claustrophobic.

The End is Near

'Wow, this is absolutely beautiful. I'm honestly speechless. This was definitely worth the travel here. You know how much I love when the sky is pink. It's absolutely fucking perfect,' Callum said, 'this is perfect, being here, surrounded by nature, how fresh the air feels. Being with you. Thank you for bringing me here.'

They sat down on the sand with their skin brushing the sand; Taylor's thick muscular arms wrapped around his petite body. To both of them, the water was peaceful. A man who looked like a nomad with long dark hair and colourful harem pants sat further afront the dune playing an acoustic guitar – strings of an unknown song. It was like the setting of a rom-com.

'I saw on the internet that it was going to be a pink sky tonight so I thought that it would be perfect to come here and see it in all of its glory. To just sit and relax because we've both been so busy with work. I suppose that's just one of the things about life. You can't always make time for yourself or your nearest and dearest. Has it been worth it?'

'Considering we missed the train twice and I've been in the worst mood possible, it was definitely worth it. Even just being here with you is worth it. I love you so much. Thanks, Tay.'

'I love you, too.' They kissed again.

They ran hand in hand down the beach until the ice cold water rubbed against their skin. Callum threw the salty water in Taylor's face, the action reciprocated. They paddled around, the chill of each other's bodies colliding in the water. It was close to freezing in the water but it felt therapeutic, Callum thought. As they continued paddling, Taylor rested the light weight of Callum's body on his knee in the water as they kissed to the sound of crashing waves, birds squawking for scraps of food, the murmur of strangers talking on the beach, crowds of people singing and shouting, and the faint volume of the man's guitar in the background.

For the next hour, the pink sky dimmed to a gloomy grey. They lay in their underwear – Callum in briefs and Taylor in boxer shorts – as the cool breeze dried their bodies before the train journey home. He felt so anxious in tight briefs but the sky had darkened so there was less visibility and Taylor's masculinity made him feel protected. Discussions flown between them about finding a two-bedroom house within their budget, Callum's plans for relaxing on his birthday in May when he would turn 23, and their important three-day trip to Lisbon for the end of June. They conversed of the possible itinerary for their trip: riding the yellow trams; eating buttery pastel de nata; drinking ruby red cocktails; visiting the Belém Tower; wandering the streets of Portugal in the urban areas to absorb the culture locals wandered past every morning. They both equally hoped that the trip abroad would bring clarity not experienced captive between the four walls of their flat. They were exhausted from laughing, swimming in the sea, kissing, and daydreaming.

The End is Near

Callum had left the hostel a month prior, citing an emergency as his reason for departing in the middle of the night, leaving his room key and a note with an unknown female receptionist. She was around 40 years old with a thick accent – Callum thought that it was Eastern European, maybe Polish or Albanian. She had luscious blonde locks that overemphasised her aquiline nose, long nostrils, and defined lower face. How bittersweet it seemed to leave HHI behind and all of the personal growth made. Memories to be cherished forever, even at his most vulnerable. Helpful Hand Initiative lived up to its name. Ian and Ed had been integral in his recovery and he owed them his life if they ever needed it. Ian called the next morning and they met for coffee so he could give a life speech to follow his dreams, always remember his power, and to never allow any abuse from Taylor. They still spoke for hours a day via text and visited each other through the week; Ian yet to meet Taylor, Callum toying whether it would ever be a good decision to mix them aspects of his life.

On the train journey home, they continued their exquisite evening with excessive laughter, reverie of the Portuguese sun, and public displays of affection. Callum rubbing Taylor's bare thigh, Taylor kissing Callum's neck. Callum noted Taylor's conversation break mid-sentence, following his gaze upwards to see a young queer man gliding through the train to the next carriage behind them. He was around the same age as him and a similar height, with dirty fake tan and bleach blonde hair. He had soft and inviting eyes but horrible fuzzy eyebrows that sat above them like thick caterpillars. The stranger laughed theatrically with his two female friends until he saw Taylor and his expression went vacant. Callum knew instantly that the person in front of them was the reason that their relationship had broken-down. He must have been the recipient of the gold bracelet – Liam.

'Hello,' the stranger said, a high-pitched voice. He was followed by two girls who looked just as unpresentable. One had yellow coloured hair with dark roots, and the other was curvy with dark brown hair and overfilled lips. Liam seemed to be the leader of the pack, stood in front of the girls

'Liam. Nice to see you mate. H-have y-you been okay?' Callum noticed the way that Taylor had stuttered when he spoke, a clear indication of guilt.

'All good, thanks. How have you been? You must be Callum. Nice to meet you.'

'Yeah, this is Callum. All good, thanks.'

'Great. Well, I'll see you later. Bye, Callum.'

'Goodbye,' Callum said nonchalantly.

They continued through the train carriage and Callum could hear muffled conversation as Liam and his cronies walked behind them. He then heard gasps, loud laughter following suit. *What a gang of idiots*, Callum's inside voice said. Taylor watched the darkness out of the train window with a tight jaw, solidifying the tension. Although Callum appreciated Taylor's attempt of suppressing the past – how could they grow pretending that the night of Christmas never happened? They both had life experiences that shaped who they were – whether it tainted the reality of who they were was a question for themselves.

'Was that him?' he asked quietly, his hand still wrapped under Taylor's.

'Ummm… yeah. Yeah, it was. I feel awkward now. Don't know why. I'm sorry, Callum. For everything I've done to hurt you in the past.'

'No need to be. Everything is going to be okay. It is what it is,' Callum said politely, 'I'm fine, by the way. Thank you for telling me the truth. I love you.' He leaned forward and kissed him. They carried on talking about their planned trip whilst browsing for clothes to wear there – the internet said June in the city was warm but a breeze cooled the evenings, influencers on TikTok recommended pants for the evening and to carry a jacket with you at all times – which resulted in Callum ordering a pair of linen pants he was unsure would be his style from his usual fitted jeans.

The End is Near

The further the train descended; the more anxiety had begun to build inside of him. Aware of Taylor's infidelity in the past, seeing Liam in real life had made everything seem melancholy and familiar. His heart rate had increased, he felt dizzy, and his brain was swirling with dark thoughts – Taylor and Liam laying together, his boyfriend caressing the face of another human, complimenting his skinny body, and fucking him until he climaxed. When they got home, he slept facing the wall, so he could feel as alone as possible without raising concerns for sleeping on the sofa as a form of respite. During his light sleep, Callum thought about what Ed would tell him to do – he envisioned them both sat in his miniscule office whilst Ed psychoanalysed the solution to his problem – and the firm answer from him would be to have an open discussion with Taylor on his anxieties.

When he woke the next morning – sleep comprised of tossing, turning, nightmares, and sweat – Callum was unsure how to approach the situation. He dreamt of Taylor having sex with Liam multiple times throughout the night, waking up continuously on ejaculation. He hoped that he would get reassurance without an argument.

'Good morning. How come you slept so far away from me last night? I turned over and you were basically hanging off the bed, you nutter,' Taylor greeted him when he woke up around 45 minutes later.

The End is Near

'Taylor, I need to speak to you about something. You know that lad that we saw on the train yesterday? Do you ever think about him? Or am I just overthinking? I'm sorry to bring it up again but I had a rough night's sleep so my brain has gone into overdrive.' He could smell Taylor's familiar body odour of musk and residue deodorant when he wrapped him up in a warm embrace.

'Callum. I promise you right now… I swear on your life, actually, I swear on everything in this fucking universe that he doesn't even cross my mind. The last time we were together… yeah… obviously. I'm not going to lie to you, he did. Now all I think about is you. I thought you knew I'd changed. There's no one else in my life except you, I'm being completely honest with you. Seeing him yesterday meant absolutely nothing to me. He's just something of the past to me now.'

'I just have my doubts sometimes. It's been hard letting you back in when you did me so wrong in the past. I know you have changed but you can't blame me for my hesitations. I just get scared in case you find somebody better and leave me. I know I probably sound silly.'

'I completely understand. If you had cheated on me, I'd always doubt myself. And you. All I can say is I'm really sorry for what I did to you in the past. I wouldn't do that to you ever again. I'm a different person, I promise you.'

'I'm trying to believe you. I did believe you until I saw him yesterday on the train. Taylor, what were you thinking? I'm nothing special... I know I'm ugly but he looked dirty.'

'You're *not* ugly. You're the most gorgeous boy I've ever laid eyes on. He was dirty, you're right.'

'Was the sex good?' Callum asked, brushing his hair across his forehead.

'I can't remember.'

'Just tell me the truth.'

'It was okay, nothing out of the ordinary. Callum, can we just stop talking about it, please? You have nothing to worry about, I promise you. I love you, and I mean that, Callum. Stop doubting me and also doubting yourself.'

'I love you too.'

They had consensual sex again, this time Taylor pulled out and came in his mouth.

It seemed bizarre to call life perfect after everything endured the past two years, but Callum thought it seemed to be. Summer was approaching which meant the sun set later, the temperature increased, and you could walk around without a jacket. There were no quarrels between them, he continued going out with Ian regularly, and was flourishing in his managerial career.

Callum had his first major dilemma as store manager when Natalie – the egotistical trouble causer – had been aggressive to customers, to the point of shouting and swearing at the elderly. He had already warned her about her conduct at work, and although she was apologetic at the time, it had seemed distinctly insincere. 'I'm sorry, mate. I've had loads of shit going on at home. My dad's a fucking wanker. Him and my mam are getting divorced so our house has been up the wall. I'll sort it out, lad. I need this job,' Natalie had said. With her pleas of forgiveness, Callum agreed to give her another chance without a disciplinary hearing.

He called her in for a second encounter at 11 o'clock with butterflies in his stomach. They had a tough discussion that lasted a paltry six minutes; Natalie telling him many times that he was the worst manager she had ever had; Callum telling her that her attitude wouldn't get her far in life; Natalie telling him that she hated him; Callum telling her that she was dismissed immediately and to hand her badge in. Their exchange ended with her slamming her lanyard down on the desk and storming out of the store with her middle finger up, claiming that she hoped the store went up in flames with him trapped inside.

Subsequently, Natalie had been dismissed and recruitment would be tasked with finding another retail assistant to fill her nameless void. His first dilemma had panned out worse than expected with Natalie's fiery mouth, but the result was to his advantage because she was gone, thankfully. He was store manager and doing an exceptional job; theft was lower since integrating a new security system; profits were at an all-time high; morale was high amongst employees. Nothing could dim his shine.

Callum realised there was a widespread poverty issue in his home city. Shoplifters in the dozens were banned from the store and the staffroom was overrun with photographs of felons caught by the CCTV and security guards. He respected the shoplifters who were strategic with their approach to thieving, the ones who understood the rota of security guards to avoid the risk of arrest.

On his way to the flat from the bus stop, he saw Wendy dragging the bins out for collection day the following morning. Four months separated from her seemed like a lifetime, and Callum wondered why he never visited since moving back into the flat with Taylor. Instant guilt crept in when he saw her posture liquify into delight when she saw his petite figure walking towards her. Large saggy breasts that bounced up and down when she lightly jogged towards him. Pink pyjamas and slippers.

'Oh, Callum! Where the fuck've you been? I haven't seen you for months. Don't tell me you're back living with Taylor... again.'

'Hi, Wend. I've missed you so much. I didn't know whether to knock at yours because I just left randomly last time. I wasn't sure whether you would want to see me. Yep, we're back together. Everything seems to be going perfect.'

'You *silly* boy. My door is always open for you. Has everything been okay between you two? Why don't you come in for a quick cuppa and we can have a catch up?'

She made him a coffee just how he liked it whilst he told her about the past four months. Beginning with the unreceived bracelet, to departing on Boxing Day morning in the freezing cold and sleeping on the streets, his stint at HHI, therapy with beautiful Ed, his friendship with Ian, his exciting new job and promotion, life with no drugs, the quiz night which resulted in him being back on the same street as Wendy, their day at the beach, and the shock of seeing Liam on the train home.

'That bloody bastard was cheating on you with somebody else and bought them a bracelet instead of giving it to you? What a horrible little fucker. Cal, why've you gone back to him? *Seriously*. You're such a smart little boy with the world ahead of you. I can't believe you are a manager – in bloody Primark, one of the busiest places in town. Congratulations! Your nan would be so proud,' she patted his left hand.

'Thank you. I'm so proud of myself and everything seems to be going well. I've been unsure what I wanted to do with my life since I ruined my degree and had basically no career prospects. I think since getting off drugs, life is amazing. When I got the job in Mike's, I realised I wanted something more customer-focused, you know? Of course it's in a completely different capacity to my last job as a carer, but it feels similar. On my feet all of the time, helping others, working on a rota with no set hours. You never know, I could be the area manager or something in the next couple of years.'

'I already know that you will be one day. Keep at it, love. The world is your oyster. So fill me in, how did you end up back with that bastard? To be fair, when he came round to the house saying you had gone missing, he seemed distraught. He was saying that he would go all of the hostels to find you.' Wendy spoke without looking at him.

'He said he went about 15 hostels looking for me. I'm glad he stuck to his word. I went out with Ian who I met at the hostel. He's the manager there, bit of a strange turn of events like. Anyways, we went to that quiz night I told you about and he got me this,' Callum showed her the necklace wrapped around his neck. Proud as ever of the pity present.

'Cal, that is gorgeous! What a nice necklace. It's the least he could do though, don't you think? Sorry to ask – have you spoken to your nan?'

'Nope. No contact at all. I've come to terms with it now. We'll never ever have a relationship again, no matter how much it does break my heart. I still think about her every day. However, I think speaking about it with my counsellor has helped me accept it. I try to not dwell on it too much, as long as she's okay and knows I'll always love her, that's all that matters to me. I know I fucked up and I should never have laid my hands on her or screamed at her, but the fact is I did. I'm a changed person now, Wend. I don't take drugs, I rarely drink, I have a good job and a lot going for me. I don't need her holding all that negativity against me for the rest of my life. It's not fair on me.'

'Okay, love. I understand. And how is Taylor being with you? Have you had two any arguments since you moved back in?' Wendy asked.

'Absolutely perfect. I couldn't fault him; he's seriously changed as a person. It's unbelievable how much he's matured. There's a two-bedroom house within our budget we're just waiting to hear back on from the estate agent. Honestly, life seems perfect. Who'd have thought? I have my doubts sometimes but I realise that's because of the past. I'm sure they'll disappear over time. He's so kind now, it's crazy. It's like something has switched inside of him.'

'That sounds... promising. I hope it stays that way.' She managed a tight smile.

'Me too, Wend. Me too.'

After they finished their mothers' meeting, hot drinks, biscuits, and jangling about the neighbours – Cathy from number 12's husband had walked out on her with a 19-year-old receptionist from work over two weeks, they had argued in the street as she threw all of his belongings out – they hugged and exchanged numbers since Callum had changed his, before he went back to the flat where Taylor had lasagne left over in the oven ready to be heated for him.

'Did you know Dave from number 12 has a tiny penis? Wendy heard Cathy shouting it the other afternoon whilst we were at work,' Callum sniggered over a fork full of creamy lasagne.

'That's information I didn't need to know about my 40-odd-year-old neighbour.'

'Do you think people in LA shout about their penis size in the street?' Callum asked, chuckling at the topic of conversation.

'I *highly* doubt it. We'll find out one day.'

One day. A dream.

The End is Near

The following Thursday, emotions raced in the flat whilst they got ready. Quiz night with Ian and Kate. Callum methodically rubbing the iron over his clothing; Taylor pacing around the flat whilst the floorboards grunted under every step. Ian had called two evenings prior, inviting him to another quiz in a local food and drinks market that had been reviewed as "intense" and "hysterical".

'Why don't you bring this fella of yours? It would be good to meet him. See what all the fuss is about,' Ian had asked over the phone.

'I'm not sure he could handle a quiz. He's not the sharpest tool in the box to be honest,' Callum laughed.

'Where is he now?'

'Next to me with his middle finger up.'

When Taylor agreed to accompany them for quiz night; questions swirled around Callum's brain about the concept of his two separate lives intertwining. Would Taylor and Ian enjoy each other's company? Would Ian bring up things from the past? Would Taylor retaliate? Would they end up brawling in the middle of town? He tried to settle his mind and not focus on the potential downfalls because what if it all went perfectly? He couldn't find a reason why it would go disastrous.

The End is Near

'Why am I nervous? I'm only going out for a drink with your mates,' Taylor said. Callum watched, reminiscent of their previous drug-infused binges. The way that Taylor would pace around the living room like a lost puppy, scooping the blinds open so he could catch a glimpse of the dealer's car headlights igniting the road. It was nice to see him worried about a simpler scenario. They continued back and forth all night, at home, on the bus, walking into the venue and meeting Ian and Kate, and when it would only be them two left at the table.

'Do you think they like me?' Taylor asked for the third time in less than half an hour.

'Taylor, seriously. They do like you. You're my boyfriend so of course they do,' Callum reassured him unsuccessfully.

'They haven't said that, though. They've just been making normal conversation and haven't said anything like that. So they definitely don't, do they?' Callum wondered whether he was now the dominant in their relationship. Had the tables turned? Callum tried all day to settle Taylor's mind but nothing seemed to work.

'Are you all right? You've been like a bag of nerves all day. They do like you but they aren't going to roll a red carpet out for you because you're here. Take it easy, Taylor. Everything's fine. They like you. I promise.' Taylor's eyes raised from Callum to behind, a nod of their arrival.

'Welcome back,' Taylor greeted them enthusiastically. Callum rolled his eyes.

'Hello, hello, hello. God, the service in here is shocking. They obviously cannot handle the influx of people in here.'

'I agree. At least the quiz is done. Eighth place, not too bad.'

'Why don't we drink these and then go to Heaven and have a dance, Taylor? I always say, you don't know a person until you have seen them on the dancefloor.'

Trailing to Heaven linked arm in arm: Kate to the left, Ian, and Callum. Taylor followed behind slowly, ill-fitted and alone. The strength of their bond was refreshing, symbolic of friendship's capability to rid all negativity in the world; satisfying the theory that the burden of love was enough to conquer all. He felt like an outcast on the journey to the club, struggling to insert himself in the conversation when handed prompts by Callum or Ian, a vacant expression when he struggled to follow the conversation, and false laughter when he blankly heard the others laughing. His mind automatically traced back to a year prior. Thinking of how rotten he had treated the person strolling in front of him. The beer and vodka he had drunk made him feel nauseous, passing drunk people on their way to another bar. Girls in short skirts, men in jeans, dogs in harnesses, and punters begging on street corners.

His mind stuck on one night in particular. Late September. He had fucked him without his consent, choking him with both hands whilst he lay inanimate and naked. He raped him. He raped him because he was aroused and would never take no for an answer. A criminal act worthy of imprisonment. An act committed against somebody he should have loved and protected.

As he walked in his thoughts, Taylor could still hear their faint conversations conjoined with roars of laughter. He felt alone, like how Callum must have felt every time he was abused. Smoking a joint after he had just came inside of him. Throwing his body on the bed and slamming the door shut, a lack of remorse for taking his lover's innocence away.

'Callum... I'm going to go home. I feel like shit. Ian and Kate, it was boss meeting you both. Have a good night you three,' Taylor said abruptly, leaving the others perplexed. He kissed Callum, shook hands with Ian, and gave Kate a gentle kiss on the cheek. Turning around, he paced quickly for the taxi rank. Callum followed him, processing the urgency to remove himself from the social setting.

'Hey, you're shaking. Is everything okay?'

'Yeah. Everything is *fine*. I just want to go home.'

The End is Near

'I'll come home with you, let me just say bye to Ian.'

'*No*! Don't. Stay out. Enjoy yourself with your mates, you deserve it. I'm fine honestly. I'm going to flag a taxi, get a takeaway on the way home and go straight to bed.'

'I'll come home with you now, shall I?' which was dismissed by Taylor, 'you're being *so* weird. Are you okay? I knew it… are you going to see someone?'

'No! Callum, no! As if you would even think that.'

'So why do you want to go home without me? You're obviously going to see someone… wow. Why the fuck did I ever trust you again?'

'Don't start me, Callum. We've had a good night. I'm not going to see anyone; I swear on your life. I'll let you track me on my phone. I'm just knackered but please stay out and enjoy yourself. I honestly can't be bothered drinking anymore and I'm in work tomorrow, too.' He gave Callum another kiss and stumbled into the back of a black taxi, giving him no chance to deliberate any further.

The torment further materialised when his ride home was accompanied by a 68-year-old widowed taxi driver named Barry who couldn't let there be silence in his cab. Barry spoke of himself; how he had previously worked as a matron in the Royal Hospital in town and then decided that the pay didn't correspond with his responsibility, so chose to work part-time as a taxi driver for Liverpool Cabs whilst claiming money from his NHS retirement pot. Although he'd had two heart attacks and the doctors advised against working nights, he liked late starts, so he didn't feel lonely in bed since the passing of his wife, and he could hear the stories of people's drunk nights out – living vicariously through the younglings. He received nothing but audible grunts from Taylor.

He stripped naked when he got to the flat, a trail of his clothes starting from his shoes at the front door to his underwear at the corner of the bed. Feeling the chill of the cold quilt over his body, he curled into the foetal position and cried for the first time in his adult life. He hated himself.

In the past when Taylor's comedown from drugs would set in, he would flip out at Callum. The repetition of it all had worn their relationship down to a skewed perception that infidelity was key to make monogamy work, or that aggressive sex could be the solution to the internalised narcissism. Intimacy had flown from his conscious mind the first time they tried their relationship; his mind fuelled with hazy anger towards Callum for reasons unknown. He worried that who he used to be was still present in their relationship, curiously thinking if Callum had been manipulated once again to fall in love with him when he could never give him what he deserved.

Was the reason they were together because of a mutually advantageous relationship that benefit both parties? Or was it down to the fact that neither of them knew no better and all they had known for over a year was each other?

Taylor struggled to compose himself through fits of tears; crying uncontrollably like a timid little child abandoned by its mother. The fear of voicing his anxieties to Callum tortured his mind, the dichotomy of support from his love mixed with the irrational fear of rejection. He wished for nothing more than his presence next to him. His arms cuddled around him, telling him that everything was going to be okay. Taylor knew that he had always craved instant gratification in the form of pleasure which was why intercourse played a pivotal role in his relationships. He wondered if his emotive state was a sign of growth or a lack of testosterone. Was he shapeshifting into a puny being? *Was his macho-persona disintegrating before their eyes?* Could he still protect himself and his lover the way he once did? He toyed with the physical support he could once provide Callum, but now it seemed that Callum did the supporting. Since moving back in together, they had become inseparable except when forced to separate for work. Their bond had grew like the Earth revolving around the sun: the Earth unable to survive without. Yet, Taylor couldn't shake off the concept that he had manipulated Callum to give their relationship another chance.

Is everythin ok? Wish u were here dancin with mex xxx

He fired a text back.

Ye babe fine xx just in bed. Enjoy urself, love you xxX

He browsed through recent memories they had made together on his camera roll. The scenic view of the Albert Dock and its stretching water, Callum's structured side profile radiating under the dying sun, his hair falling on his forehead in an arranged mess. He zoomed in on his soft lips. Lips that had been wrapped around the shaft of his penis countless times. Continuing to scroll through his camera roll, he saw photographs of their fingers locked, a selfie kissing, the image of a full moon they sat under and spoke about their future, a picture of the ice cream they bought, decorated with sherbet and raspberry sauce.

He was incapable of sleep as his mind went back to the past and forth to the future. The fear that how he tortured his love in the past would result in negative karma for the future. His heart being broken and left abandoned for good. The fear seemed imminent. The end is near, Taylor thought.

He lay wide awake when Callum burst through the door, stumbling home early hours: tripping around the flat, coughing loudly, and humming a tune that Heaven must have played.

'Tay, are you awake? Please wake up!' Callum shouted louder than anticipated.

'Fuck off, Callum, I'm definitely awake now. Do you want to be any louder? The noise of you is like a herd of elephants.' Taylor could hear Callum removing each individual piece of clothing – socks, pants, t-shirt, until finally, his underwear.

'Did I wake you up? I'm so sorry, *babe*.' He was breathing heavily and reeked of alcohol.

'No. I was awake anyway.'

'How come you are still awake? You left me hours ago.'

'I've been tossing and turning. Nothing in particular has kept me awake. I think it's all of the ale drank. It's been a while.' *Rapist, rapist, rapist*, his internal voice chimed. 'Cal, can I ask you a question?'

'Ummm... y-yeah, sure.'

'Do you forgive me for what I did? Like... honestly forgive me? Or do you still think about it? I don't just mean cheating... I mean, you know... other things.'

'Like raping me?' Callum asked, more blunt than he expected from him.

There was a thick ribbon of fog lingering outside. The street lamp in their front was invisible through the grey. Raindrops pattered against the glass window and the interior of the flat was dark and eery.

'Is that why you went home early?'

'No. Well… yeah. Maybe. I don't know. I've been feeling a bit down recently. I just feel like… I don't know, to be honest. It's hard for me to explain. I think I feel guilty. Guilty that you've given me another chance when I never deserved it,' Taylor spoke quietly, 'since not taking drugs, my emotions are all over the place. I think about everything I've done in the past – even before you. The way I treated my mum and dad, the mates I made, fucking everything up in school. Do you ever get like that?'

'Sometimes. We all get like that at times and it's completely normal to have ups and downs. Don't forget, you've been taking drugs since a very young age. Think of all of them years' worth of partying that's in your system. No, I don't think about our past, really. You're a completely different person.'

Taylor smiled, 'really? That's just eased my mind. I still think I'm the worst person in the world.'

'I love you. Look where we are now. Yeah, I did say that I would never forget, but hand on my heart, I have, or I'm trying to. You've changed so much. It is honestly unbelievable how much you have changed. It's like you're a completely different person from when I first met you. You finally have a heart, like the tin man in *The Wizard of Oz* wanted.'

'I love you, Cal. Thanks for reassuring me.'

Both slept well that night. Taylor dreamt a recurring dream – it was one of his favourites – trapped in a supermarket in the midst of a zombie apocalypse. Callum was there, his parents, his auntie, Agnes, Adrian, Stacey, other non-playable characters, and strangely, Cathy and Dave from number 12. It was full of gory details and heads being decapitated by kitchen knives. Whenever he had that dream, something good had happened, or was about to happen. Maybe it was the realisation that his partner had finally forgiven him.

Callum's birthday came around fast. He turned 23 on the 17th of May having pub dinner surrounded by his favourite humans. Taylor, Ian, and Wendy completed his social circle. Taylor bought him some clothes for their holiday the following month. On the Saturday after his special day, they decided to complete a spring clean of the flat to decide which furniture needed selling – Taylor wouldn't donate it to the charity shop as they desperately needed the money – or which empty parts of the flat needed furnishing.

The End is Near

CHAPTER NINE

International tourists and the local Portuguese marvelled at the unfamiliar display of amusement unfolding before them. Two queer British tourists embroiled in an alcohol-charged shouting match; an unusual and irritating sight in the tranquil neighbourhood of Bairro Alto: the heart of Lisbon. Known for its viewpoints and romantic architecture, the ecru and orange coloured walls were beautiful against the backdrop of a clear teal sky. Quaint apartments above popular local restaurants buzzed with life; flora hung from balconies above; washing hung from tiny balconies; yellow graffiti was painted onto soft pink walls; unsteady cobblestones on the ground; succulent fruit and vegetables outside local produce stores. The city was quiet and peaceful, except for them.

'You're a horrible bastard, you know. An absolute *bastard*. You have always got to make everything about you. *Always*.' Callum spoke loudly, expansively flapping his arms through the warm summer breeze.

'Callum... I haven't done anything wrong. I said, "I feel ashamed that you're dancing in the middle of the street", I was only joking! You've caused an absolute scene when I was fucking joking.'

The cause of their most reason squabble was that they had been drinking since 11 o'clock in the morning – now an unfamiliar habit but a decision they decided on to cure the previous days' hangover – with Callum a lot drunker than Taylor. Intoxicated, Callum decided to dance in the middle of the street to a busker singing in Portuguese. Tensions reached boiling point between both. Taylor made a joke, and Callum – to the surprise of Taylor, although recognisable from the past – detonated like a bomb.

'Please do not even attempt to downplay it to make me look like a fool. I was dancing, having a joke, and you've caused a scene, dragging me away and shouting at me in the middle of the street.' Callum had not noticed the onlookers watching. Expressions of awe, disgust, and amusement flooding the spirits surrounding them.

'Callum, I never dragged you away. I lightly pulled you away and made a joke so that we could carry on walking and actually go and explore. I was laughing at you dancing. Why would I be laughing for any other reason?'

'Because you're horrible. That's why you were laughing at me. You dragged me, Taylor! Don't lie!'

'I never dragged you,' Taylor said, attempting to dismantle the animosity, apprehensive of the numerous strange faces observing them. 'We've been planning this trip for months and all we've done since being here is argue constantly! You need to liven up... look around us.' The shops visible were a bookstore with 70% off selected books in English, three restaurants, two wine bars, a laundrette, a nail salon, a bakery with perfectly crafted butter croissants, a charity shop, and a trinket store, housing thousands of vintage artefacts. 'I'm sorry, Cal. I honestly don't think I did anything wrong. You took it the wrong way and then went off on me.'

'You're looking for an argument again! Why can't you just apologise?' Callum said.

Taylor exhaled sharply before he spoke, 'okay. I'm sorry. Can we please just try to fucking enjoy ourselves? Seriously. I didn't mean anything bad. I was laughing with you – emphasis on with – because of your dancing. I would never laugh at you, Cal. I always want to support you. We've only got another day left here before we return to normality. Please, let's just enjoy it in peace.' *Silence between them. Prolonged silence. Exhausting silence. Huffing. Puffing. More silence.*

'You're right. I'm sorry. I don't know what's come over me recently. I feel dead anxious on this trip. I wanted to make sure everything was perfect but I'm overthinking the situation and actually making it worse.'

The solution to all of their problems was physical touch. Taylor traced his hands down Callum's spine; feeling the heat of the sun absorbing into his black linen shirt worn slightly unbuttoned, a pale chest on display. The stimulation that aroused the both of them through touch destroyed every problem in the world. Wars ended, natural disasters stopped, poverty ceased.

'No more alcohol for a while. Let's sober up with a coffee,' Taylor offered.

They walked through the vibrant streets until they arrived at a coffee shop, taking in the views of urban Lisbon and the multiple styles of architecture ranging from neoclassical to gothic – all magically complimenting one another. Callum occasionally stumbled. Narrow apartments sat nestled between rows of stores and restaurants – an inviting and united city. More rows of terraced apartment blocks were slotted between parks and walkways for people to travel around; Lisbon interconnected as one large municipality. They looked in the windows of every shop they passed, even if it was the same pair of women's heels that five previous stores had sold. They were indecisive with their coffee shop choice and eventually settled for one called Lisboa Coffee Lab, in the Baixa district, that had a small outdoor seating area in the back which trapped the natural sunshine like a sauna. The shop was dark wood with sage painted walls and fresh pastries and homemade bread on display. The first fixture on arrival was a large vintage record player and ceiling high bookshelves stuffed with vinyl of many genres from hip-hop to classical, pop to country. They both stood browsing through the selection, marvelling at records of Lauryn Hill next to Kenny Rogers, next to Aretha Franklin, next to Elisabeth Schwarzkopf. They both ordered a caramel latte and an almond croissant to share before dinner. The mood in Lisboa Coffee Lab was soft and calm; the undertone of muttered conversation mixed with Bob Dylan.

Taylor ordered them another round of two coffees. The female barista who served him was beautiful. No older than 20 years of age with ashy blonde hair that sat below her breasts, glass skin that glistened under the fluorescent lighting, soft make up blended perfectly on her face in the right shade for her fair Scandinavian skin. She wore an industrial white shirt underneath her grey apron, with "Ingrid" on her name tag. He was curious about her ethnicity, if she was not Portuguese – how had she ended up working at a coffee shop there? Taylor watched how she moved behind the counter robotically, picking utensils up without having to look where anything was. He said thanks for his coffee and left it at that.

The End is Near

They decided to hire a private guided tour on the back of a rickshaw to guide them from the port of Lisbon, through the quaint neighbourhoods of the city, to the base of the Sintra mountains and back, for a sum of €80. The tour was instructed by Charlotte, an expat from France, who had moved to Portugal in 2008 following the breakdown of her 11 year marriage. Charlotte still had her native tongue which meant her English was slightly broken at times. She struggled to understand some of the terms used by Taylor and Callum, their Scouse accents thick. Regardless of the language barrier, her aura was infectious and they decided on her within ten seconds. She spoke with her hands and face, always animated from pride, to disgust, to confusion.

She knew minor details about buildings that weren't stops on the tour – 'I know that the composition of that building was produced with bricks that no longer exist.' – 'I have read countless times that a certain Spanish aristocrat had a sex dungeon in that building to the left.' – that made her feel authentic. She liked her job, but most importantly, she respected her clientele.

'I never take this job for granted. I get to explore the most beautiful city in the world and you pay me for the luxury.' Regardless of their withering budget, they tipped her an additional €20 for her guidance, gave her a five star review on an excursion website, and promised to recommend her to anybody who visited.

The finale of their tour included a small picnic at the foot of the Sintra mountains on private grounds of a multimillionaire's holiday home that he allowed tourists to use free of charge. The mountains stood large in the background of their scenic feast, surrounded by large trees, beautiful sculptures, an oversized fountain that produced the most clear blue water, and perfectly planted flora in an array of colours. Charlotte waited nearby to allow them more intimacy – although with ten other people in the gardens – and refused to eat even when they urged for her company. The picnic consisted of fresh bread, butter, strawberries, scones, and two cupcakes.

Taylor watched in admiration at the laughter that erupted from Callum when he told him a ridiculous joke about strawberries. How Callum covered his nicotine stained teeth when he laughed. His cheeks grew pink in colour. There was a small vein that stuck out above his left eyebrow when any sort of strong emotion spread across his face, and he convulsed back and forth, smacking his hands off whatever proximate when laughing. In that instance, it was Taylor's bicep victim to Callum's light touch.

'Stop staring at me, I hate the way you look at me when I'm laughing,' Callum said, attempting to compose himself. He hated the vulnerability of laughter, even though a natural emotion incomparable to any other feeling. He could feel his lover's eyes still on him, unable to withdraw his stare. Mesmerised in the sorrow of his ugliness. Yes, he was hard-working, and yes, he was as kind and gracious as he could be, but Callum knew he lacked any physical attractiveness. He believed that his body was too thin, his teeth were yellow and crooked, and he had a disproportionate nose.

'I can't help it,' Taylor admitted.

'*Stop*. Please.'

'Tay, look how cute that dog is!' he said, attempting to deflect the conversation to another topic. A small miniature fluffy dog walked past outside the gate of the garden but regardless, Taylor's eyes never moved. 'Why do you actually stare at me so much when I'm laughing? You know how uncomfortable it makes me feel and you carry on doing it. Please stop.'

'I honestly can't. Your laugh is intoxicating. You look beautiful when you laugh. It's my favourite emotion on you,' Taylor said.

'Why though? I hate it. I wish I could just laugh internally and not have an expression on my face. I look so ugly.'

'That would be boring though, wouldn't it? Laughter makes the world go round. You're the most beautiful boy on this planet.'

'I love you so much. Thank you for the best holiday. Our first holiday together. I hope we make so many more amazing memories together,' Callum kissed his cheek.

'I love you more, baby.'

After their rickshaw ride and goodbyes to Charlotte, Taylor and Callum rode the metro to the Lisbon Art Museum, although neither were particularly concerned for art or the ambiguous and pretentious meaning behind paintings. The museum was nestled on thousands of square feet of land with alluring gardens and even a small seasonal fairground composed of a miniature wooden rollercoaster, a merry-go-round, and others at the front of the building. The museum was directly opposite the dark metro station, less than a kilometre walk to the front entrance of the grand building. The land was green. Women sat under the shade of trees reading poetry, amateur photographers took pictures of the grass, dogwalkers and their furry friends roamed freely through the breeze.

The building of the Lisbon Art Museum was a colossal Georgian style building with its original features, except refurbished stained glass windows all over, evenly spaced apart. A large orangery was attached to the museum that appeared to be a bar and restaurant; flocks of people sat gossiping with a live singer seemingly harmonising with a violinist.

Something both were obsessed with was the art of people-watching. Observing how people from all different walks of life were experiencing the same moment differently. Conversations were different. Emotions were different. Worries were different. Sometimes, Taylor and Callum would go to restaurants or coffee shops and eavesdrop on the conversations around them. In the past, they had overheard talks of failing marriages because of their husbands infidelity with men, failed IVF treatments and the possibility of surrogacy, illegal drug rings, and international prostitutes based in London. The joy and anticipation they felt on sitting down – whether it be for food at a restaurant, or on a train journey – and overhearing a deep discussion from members of the general public was the epitome of happiness.

They bought their tickets inside the foyer and made their way around the museum, browsing through the network of art on display. There was a Peruvian exhibition on for the month of June at the museum which explored the development of Peru and its independence through a journey of time. Callum noted that the brushstrokes of one particular painting were so fine that you had to be less than an inch away to see every different colour. There was a famous painting – by an artist they didn't know – at the museum that hundreds congregated around; making it improbable for smooth transition from one gallery to another.

Callum fell in love with a particular painting depicting a young black woman breastfeeding her son in a dimly lit room whilst people looked in through the windows with dismay across their faces. Callum enjoyed the painting because he thought that it showed an accurate depiction of breastfeeding in modern society, still somewhat frowned upon and sexualised by men, even though a natural act. Taylor liked it because the woman's breasts were large.

As a gift, Callum bought a keyring and fridge magnet to use as a reminder of their adventures to Lisbon – tens of memories encapsulated in the trinkets. They had an overly expensive lunch consisting of two glasses of prosecco and pasta sat in the transparent glass restaurant of the museum; watching the green trees of the gardens flutter in the warm breeze. They failed to understand anyone's conversations due to the language barrier, except one Welsh couple who didn't talk about much else other than their three-day weekend in the Portuguese capital and how the weather had been.

'So what did you think of the museum?'

'I found it interesting. However, it was a tiny bit boring. All I was thinking of was what to eat afterwards. I hate that they don't tell you about the meaning behind the paintings so you're expected to stare at a squiggly line painted on a canvas and automatically know that it's a nod to their great grandparent who died during World War II,' Callum admitted. Taylor nodded.

'Thank you for everything, Cal. I've had a lovely little trip with you.'

'Me too. Sorry for being horrible to you before,' Callum said.

'It's okay – you've already apologised anyway.'

'I know but I am sorry.'

'You're always horrible to me,' Taylor said, grinning. The laughter started again. The same expression he had desperately tried to hide had surfaced; exposing his imperfections. He couldn't stop laughing, but for once in his life, he never wanted to. Let him look at my ugly laughing face, Callum thought to himself. His laughter made Taylor start and he knew as long as he could make him laugh, they were destined for a happy ending.

They had decided to continue the night in a gay bar less than half a kilometre away from their hotel called All About Love. It was the only one on Google with reviews and had also been there the previous night, therefore knowing what to expect. It was small, with pride flags of all different sizes hung from the walls and ceiling, rough wooden furniture, and bubble gum pop songs on a continuous loop from the minute the doors opened until closing.

They did all they could to seclude themselves away in the furthest corner of the bar, though unsuccessfully. After a while, an overweight lesbian with blue and green hair like a peacock came over and sat down, sipping a bottle of Portuguese wheat beer. 'How are you both finding Lisbon?'

'We're having a good time, thanks. Are you from here?'

'Yes, I have lived in Lisbon all of my life. The city of dreams, in my opinion,' she said.

What they thought would be a short conversation turned into a night full of dancing with Freya and her friend Will. Will was from Cheshire and had moved to Lisbon three years ago to become an English teacher, due to a better work-life balance and weather. Will had recently broken off an engagement with his ex – who had fled back to the UK following their break up – so was attempting to be as haphazard as possible. They never arrived back to their hotel until four in the morning, something both regretted.

'I can't believe we stayed out that late when we've got the longest fucking day possible,' Taylor said the next morning, roaming around the airport with bloodshot eyes and a ghostly complexion, similar to that of rigor mortis. 'That's genuinely ruined my whole holiday, being this hungover… in the airport… one of the worst places known to man. I'm blaming you for my own sanity.'

'How nice were they that we met last night. I love meeting unexpected people like that. Will was a bit of a nuisance but we'll let him off.'

'I agree. It's a shame we didn't get their numbers. He was definitely into you,' Taylor joked.

'It's a shame I only have eyes for you.'

'Another trip to Portugal soon then?'

'Let's explore the world first. The world is our oyster now, baby.' They shared a small kiss on the lips and then slept for the full duration of the flight – with Taylor's head resting on Callum's shoulder – until the air hostess woke them to check their seatbelts for landing. They spoke minimally for the rest of the journey home, both incapacitated and too restless to converse. They knew each other's boundaries and that there was no necessity to make small talk when unnecessary.

When they arrived home, they left their baggage in the hall, unable to face unpacking until the following day. Simultaneously, they jumped on the bed, fully clothed and exhausted. After a couple of small innocent kisses, Callum glided himself on top of his partner's corpse-like body and began to grind on his pelvis, attempting to resuscitate him back from the grave of a hangover. Their surrounding was a bedroom filled with dirty laundry, clothes they never packed draped on the floor, empty water bottles, and dust. Outside was a humid June.

'I'm tired, Cal. Maybe another time.'

'So am I. But let's finish this trip in the best way possible.' Taylor's lip bled when Callum had attempted to seductively kiss him, biting his lip until the skin had ripped off; crimson red blood dripping from his wound. The blood had alerted Taylor when he gazed up at Callum who had stained lips like a new shade of ruby lipstick. 'I'm so sorry. I got excited. I've ruined it, haven't I?'

'Jesus, Callum. How hard did you bite me? Your lips are bright red. You must be ravenous,' he wiped away blood with the back of his hand and moved to the bathroom to clean the wound with tepid water. When he arrived with a damp tissue, Callum attempted to nurse his wound with his fingers. 'It's okay, Cal. You're rubbing my lip too hard.'

'I'm such a fucking idiot. Why did I even bother to try and initiate sex? I feel embarrassed. I've ruined everything.'

'Callum! Fuck. You are going to make my lip bleed even more! Stop it!' Taylor saw the expression on Callum's face and attempted to initiate forgiveness by leaning in for a kiss. Dismissed. Callum left the room with a slam of the bedroom door and a loud scream. A meltdown was on the horizon – like times when Taylor had moved the remote from his side of the sofa and Callum smashed two plates and a glass, or another time when he had hit Taylor over the head with an empty bottle because he told him to stop smoking all of the cigarettes – and it needed to be dealt with quickly and efficiently to avoid catastrophic consequences.

Hunched over the sofa with his face nestled in his small hands was the position Taylor found him in. 'Cal, come on. What's up?'

'No, leave me alone! I can't do this anymore!' Callum stormed through the flat.

'Do what?'

'This, Taylor. Us. Me and you. You and me. This needs to end.'

Callum had begun to kick at the cabinet that their bedroom TV rested on, the oak shaking under the strength of his vicious blows, violently kicking until he could only focus on causing pain to the woodwork. His foot broke through the wood and the bottom drawer fell to the floor with a thud, hung loose like a thread. Once he completed his mission of causing destruction, he began his next, which involved kicking and punching at the thin bedroom wall. It took a mere two seconds until the bare plaster underneath the thin and bumpy wallpaper was exposed to the naked eye. Callum's meltdown was alien, although once recurrent. Taylor stood still, watching him with trepidation. He continued to throw his fists around the room, violently hitting the walls, smashing a lamp, and throwing shoes from the floor to the wardrobe. Taylor thought he was crazy but that's what trauma does to a person.

'Callum. What's happened? You need to calm down,' Taylor spoke quietly, carefully, and apprehensively. 'Callum! Stop ruining *my* fucking flat!' Taylor shouted, failing in his pursuance of peace. Callum had continued to punch heavily against the walls of the council flat, revealing the fragile foundations that held the property together.

There was a musky smell emerging from behind the flimsy walls. Suddenly, Callum's eyes shot towards Taylor and fixated on him queerly.

'Your flat? Wow. Your fucking flat? As if I don't fucking pay for literally half of everything. And I mean half down to the penny. Your fucking flat. You're one disrespectful *bastard*.' Callum oozed with fury.

'I didn't mean it like that, Cal. Sorry.'

'Get over yourself, Taylor. You're so pathetic now. Seriously. You're such a fucking girl now. A couple of months ago you would've just slapped me across the face. Now, I pussyfoot around you like you're a fucking toddler.'

'Just go to bed and we'll speak in the morning.'

'Are you actually telling me what to do? You're not my fucking parent.'

'Callum, seriously. Stop it.'

'You're a cunt and I deserve better than you.'

'Why do you deserve better than me? What have I actually done wrong?'

Callum explained to Taylor in depth about what annoyed him. He claimed he was a liar and a cheater, suffering from narcissistic personality disorder, and all of his family and friends hated him and their relationship. He questioned why he ever gave him another chance, how their future was going to be, and the worry of whether he would ever cheat on him again.

'Where the hell has all of this even come from? We were having a belter holiday and now this. You're bizarre, you know that, Callum.'

'Sometimes things just build up. You have to release it all at some point. I'm drained. Exhausted, to be honest. With everything. I need someone who loves me in other ways than just telling me they do. Unfortunately, you don't. Sometimes I do wonder why I ever gave you another chance. As bad as it sounds, sorry, I can't help my thoughts.'

'Okay. Why did you give me another chance? Fuck off, Callum. You seemed to have been happy to have given me one until five minutes ago when you started acting like a psychopath for no reason. Seriously, go to bed, Callum. You're just fucking annoying me now.'

'Rapist.'

Taylor's hand collided hard with the soft skin of his cheek until Callum could taste the familiar metallic taste of blood in his mouth. He felt a sense of happiness that the man he once fell in love with was still there underneath the façade. A real man. An abuser. Callum could still feel the heat from his punch when his skin was met with another blast to the cheek.

'Don't fucking call me that ever again,' Taylor demanded. 'You do not get to call me that! You are a *horrible, ugly, vile* human being!' Taylor bellowed his words with saliva mounting at the corners of his thin mouth, like a rabid drug addict.

Callum noticed how small he felt in front of Taylor. A moment of anger had exhibited past techniques. He recounted previous fights they had when Taylor would strike him until his body was battered, unable to move for hours with bruises covering his body. The way he would rape him until he felt like a vulnerable little child who had been groomed, or a trafficking victim on board the back of a lorry. His comments had caused a seismic shift in their relationship, from happiness to past trauma. Observing the rage brewing in Taylor was something he had not witnessed in a while; his fragile and caring boyfriend had disappeared, and he was the causal effect.

'You know how fucking guilty I feel about the past and you are bringing it up out of spite!'

'Is it not the truth?'

'Callum, seriously. Leave me the fuck alone or I will punch you.'

After a moment of silence when Callum felt too scared to talk, Taylor slammed his hands down heavily onto the wooden furnishings of the bedroom that made an echoing noise throughout the entirety of the small flat. Callum was too afraid to insult him again in case he murdered him with his bare hands.

'I actually can't do this anymore, Taylor. I'm sorry. You're scaring me.'

'Me neither. I'm done too. You are boring and *pathetic*. I have done nothing but prove to you that I'm a different person, Callum.'

Whilst Callum may have agreed with the testament, his sudden outburst in retaliation to his comments – that he never meant, his neurodevelopmental disorder made it impossible to effectively manage every social scenario – seemed to be an inconceivable threat that eradicated the loving memories made over the past months.

'I'm leaving. I've had enough of this. This will never work out and it's not healthy for either of us to continue trying to make it work. I apologise for being nasty and causing a big argument but I think both of our reactions have shown us that this will never ever work out. No matter how hard we try or how well we think we're getting on.'

They were now stood close, gazing at the mirrored image they saw of themselves in each other. An image of vulnerability, anger, exhaustion, desperation. Callum knew that he needed to leave, but leaving would be more time lost. The existential crisis of a relationship was solemn – the balancing act of desire and fury. A flimsy diorama of security. Was this truly the end, or was this an extension of time out of the cynical fear of loneliness that left lovers in fear? The silence between them was deafening. The capacious feeling in a flat that always seemed claustrophobic was nauseating.

'Callum, are you okay? Don't leave, please. I don't want you to go again. I'm sorry for reacting the way that I did. You have every right to doubt me. I promise you that I have changed. Please don't go.' Callum's cheek was still warm when Taylor placed his hands on his skin and the guilt flooded him with regret. Callum realised that Taylor's touch could not cure the sickness inside. Incurable trauma was impossible to forget. He opened the wardrobe and began to unsystematically throw clothing onto the bed. A single item of clothing soon multiplied to piles of t-shirts, pants, and shoes.

'What're you doing?' Taylor asked. He asked again when he received no response from Callum, who continued to navigate the room, pulling toiletries from the broken drawers, socks from the bedside table, and chargers from the plug sockets.

'I'm leaving, Taylor. This time for good. I don't know where I'll go, but I need to leave before it gets too late,' Callum responded, not lifting his gaze. Terrified that one look at his eyes would make him want to stay forever.

'You know what, just go then! I don't need a big song and dance about it. I'm tired, I'm going to sleep on the sofa. See you later, mate.'

Within thirty minutes, he had completely cleared all of his belongings into an organised mess on one side of the bedroom. Clothes piled high with a washbag of toiletries the pièce de résistance of his cluttered possessions. After realising he didn't want to spend another night homeless like Christmas, Callum decided to sleep in their bed, Taylor on the sofa. He slept terribly; anxious at what the future could hold.

The next morning, Callum woke with the sun shining through the curtains of the bedroom window. He lay nestled in the crisp cotton cover, the distinguishable siren of birds tweeting and Taylor's faint snoring on the sofa the only exclamations of life.

He quickly drafted his thoughts on a scrap of paper. A simple piece of paper.

Taylor,

I'm sorry to do this again.

Leaving you like this is not how I intended. I need to do this for both of us. I'm sorry for arguing last night after a beautiful weekend away. I'm sorry for what I said about the past. It was spiteful and fuelled with hatred.

I shouldn't have been so cruel when you have been so kind to me. Sadly, although I forgive you, I clearly haven't forgotten. Sorry for yesterday and thank you for the best trip. I wish you the best of luck, please never forget me.

I will come and pick up all my stuff soon.

I love you forever and always.

Callum xxx

He left the note on the centre of the bed and left the flat urgently – an oversized backpack his only belonging. His future scarily uncertain.

When he left the flat and headed east, past the rows of archaic flats, Wendy's house, shops, and the estate, he never looked back. Not even once. To turn around and glance at what he was leaving would give him an opportunity to turn around, apologise, and resume his current lifestyle.

He needed something different. He needed change. He needed himself. A new chapter, *without him.*

CHAPTER TEN

Taylor

Sitting in the squalor that was once his most prized possession, he sat with a notepad and calculator, totalling how much money had been spent on cocaine within the past month. £2,950 from what he could remember. Sometimes splurges of a few grams for £300 a night if one of his many dealers were fond enough to do a deal. £2,950 seemed an impossible sum for him. He had never had that much money in his bank account, so how he afforded the break up blues was mindboggling. The £2,950 didn't even cover the alcohol drank, or the cigarettes and weed smoked. Further factors not mentally prepared to endure. He lost his job at Milton's two weeks after Callum left him. His body was unable to cope with the loss of his soulmate. He hadn't attended his workplace since pre-Lisbon and had no intention of ever returning, which resulted in his dismissal sent via P45 in the mail.

He watched as his phone rang on the dining table – his mother calling again, the fourth time that day. He avoided answering, resenting the lecture she would give him about the damage caused to his relationship with Callum. Pauline had left him two voicemails the day before, he never responded.

'Taylor... I know you two have split up but I have kindly given you £600 and I am yet to see it back in my bank account when you told me you would be paid the day after. I have banged on your bloody flat door and no answer. I have called you nonstop and you let it ring out. Can you just call me please, love? I'm getting worried,' was the first.

'I have just been talking to your auld man. Why did I ever agree to give you that money? I knew you would be back on drugs. I have willingly fed your addiction. What a fucking mother I am! *Ha*. You are 30 years old in two months, *grow up*. I wish I never had you as a son sometimes... you do know that? 29 years of age and still causing me nothing but fucking grief,' was the second.

An image formed in his mind of his mother stood near the back door of his childhood home, a cigarette hung from her mouth, disgraced by the wrongdoings of her evil son. However, Taylor thought she had seemed to forgive the way his alcoholic father had abused her in recent years. He still remembered the black eye on Christmas Day that she tried to conceal underneath her foundation.

The key symptom of his depressive state was losing the man he thought was his world. Therefore, the conclusion was that life wouldn't be worth living alone. If he went to see a shrink, he realised that they would lie and say it would get better. The epicentre of his universe had shattered and for the rest of his life to not fall apart would be a transgression of science. He lit another cigarette – his eighth in just over an hour – dwelling in self-pity; loathing the continuation of another lonely day. The previous time they broke up was hard. He remembered turning to meaningless sex with strangers when caught in the act of infidelity, followed by another smack in the face when Liam abandoned him too. His temper in work had made Adrian send him home for days so he could attempt to compose himself without brawling with innocent customers. Retrospectively, he envied his strength during that time. Now, weakness consumed every bone in his body.

The day that he died would be the best day of his life: one he dreamt of.

In 72 hours, the only thing that had passed Taylor's lips were instant microwave noodles and a bar of chocolate. His BMI, metabolism, and build meant that he craved at least 3,000 calories a day to ensure his body could function efficiently. The heartbreak was starting to take a toll on his physical health, too. He felt weak and dizzy when he stood up. Taylor lit another cigarette whilst deep in imagination, his past stable mental health part of the reverie.

The End is Near

'You have left me with *nothing*! I've got no one now because of you!' Taylor shouted so loud that he could feel the vibrations transcend through the flat. The only other noise was from the archaic bathroom pipes that growled aggressively. He continued to shout, but it made his head pulsate. More pressure began to form in his skull.

'Is everything okay in there?' A strange voice called from outside of the flat. It was soft, male, and sounded like an older gentleman.

With the calling came a faint knock at the front door – they tapped lightly but repeatedly – and it took a while for Taylor to realise that the voice emanating was his old, strange neighbour Graham. Graham lived across the block from him on his own with a small white Bichon Frisé called Bobbins. He was mid to late 50s with thin grey hair, a widow's peak hairline, a slim build that made him look like a serial killer, and haunting eyes that observed you for long periods of time. They both always thought that he was gay – Taylor was sure whilst Callum never liked to judge a book by its cover – but Taylor argued that his gaydar – the intuitive ability as a homosexual to know a person's sexual orientation – had never failed him before. A dog called Bobbins, sexual innuendos, and wearing a bright pink apron were all facts to support his observation.

'Hello? Just checking that everything is okay in there,' Graham called out again.

The End is Near

'Do me a favour and fuck off knocking on my door,' Taylor said.

'Are you okay? I heard shouting,' Graham asked politely.

'Leave me alone, you freak. Leave me alone before I come out there and kick your dog down the stairs,' Taylor inhaled a long drag of his cigarette.

'Excuse me! I have a good mind to report you to the housing. You're like a bloody lunatic in there. I want nothing but peace in this shithole and you seem to cause all of the problems!'

He heard Graham's front door slam and knew that he had been left alone. There was nobody at all who wanted to help him now.

Taylor lit another cigarette and watched a repeat of old Eastenders on the TV, noting only two cigarettes left and no money to buy more. It seemed that his life was on a continuous downward spiral, ranging from no boyfriend, to no family, to no friends, to no money, to no desire to change any of these circumstances. It was the middle of the afternoon and he was not motivated to do anything except drown his sorrows in alcohol.

'You're such a fucking girl now.'

'You're a cunt and I deserve better than you.'

'Rapist.'

Taylor remembered how perplexed he felt when Callum thrust insults upon him for no apparent reason. He bit his lip until it bled – which he forgave him for – but the meltdown that followed was something unexpected. Taylor wondered if he reacted differently – maybe he could have pretended to like the burning sensation from his lip when first plucked with his teeth – that Callum would still be there and he wouldn't be lonely. They would both be at work, earning money to pay the bills and to save for their next trip. They eventually decided that Rome would be the next place they visit. Callum thought it would be full of history from the Colosseum to the Trevi fountain, which Taylor agreed upon.

He had done all he could to dispose of every trace of him. Every photograph and text message in his phone had gone into the recycling bin, he had binned all of his belongings, and told his few family and friends not to discuss him again. However, indications of his longing presence always came back – he found a pair of his jeans at the bottom of the wardrobe two days prior; deciding to set them on fire in the back garden instead of disposing them in the bin as a sane person would. He thought that setting them on fire would set him free as the cheap jeans burnt into ashes in front of him. He failed in his quest and received a complaint from one of the downstairs neighbours for air pollution and the lingering stench of smoke throughout their flat.

The End is Near

The universe worked in mysterious ways, Taylor thought to himself. If you looked close enough you could see signs in places least expected. A stop sign that caught your eye more than usual could be perceived as a sign to stop criticising yourself. The different walking route could lead you to a new person and the beginning of something special. Just as the universe worked – which was miraculously – Taylor remembered that he had a gram of coke stored in the kitchen cupboard in a letter from the bank telling him to pay his overdraft. Methodically, he laid two heaped lines of white powder all over the kitchen worktop; using a knife to separate them into thick, uneven, parallel lines. He hoovered both up in less than ten seconds. The burning sensation on his nose faded too quickly: a sign of overuse since Callum's departure. After the failed attempt of escapism, Taylor decided to go to bed and masturbate, his usual routine after snorting cocaine. His sexual identity had changed since Callum left him: romance now a catalyst for depression and violent unrealistic adult films were treated as an opioid. The last image stuck in his brain whenever he came was one of Callum's naked body.

His hygiene had reached peak repulsion, bacteria from previous loads of semen lingered within his abdominal hair. His hair was greasy, his armpits reeked, and wax had built up in his ears. However, Taylor continued to turn a blind eye to his life seemingly deteriorating. Cigarettes, alcohol, cocaine, weed, and masturbating seemed to be all he knew. He was incapacitated to complete anything productive, his sorrows too heavy a burden to function as a living organism. His orgasm had exhausted him and he fell asleep until five the next morning, the seven missed calls from his mum and dad ringing through like a lullaby whilst he floated away to a land of forgotten love with Callum.

After hours of restlessness, he eventually fell back to sleep until late in the afternoon. It was the start of August in the UK and the climate was hot which made the flat nauseating even when the windows had been left open throughout the night. Pools of sweat formed across the cotton sheets of the bed when Taylor woke to the sound of his phone ringing for the umpteenth time. There was no caller ID on the phone which he was reluctant to answer but he did after the second ring, hoping that it wasn't one of his parents he had been desperately attempting to avoid.

'Hello?' Taylor answered the phone, monotone.

'Where the fuck is my money? You little queer,' was the greeting Taylor received from the unknown caller. His languid brain could not co-operate who was on the other end of the line. The voice sounded familiar but no name sprung to mind because his memory had spiralled into decay from too much booze and cocaine.

'Did you hear what I just fucking said? Where the fuck is my money? You little *queer*.'

'Who is that?' Taylor asked quietly, almost a silence.

'You know who it is. It's TJ, you little tramp. Watch me put a knife in you if you don't have my money with me by the end of the day.' TJ responded with a thick Scouse accent filled with ferocity. He was an old childhood friend who seemed pleased to hear from Taylor – a ghost from his past – wanting ten grams of cocaine the weekend before. When he arrived at the flat and requested the money, Taylor informed him that he would be paid the day after and would wire the money to his bank account as soon as he had it. TJ agreed to his request and sent him the details of his girlfriend's bank account. After numerous unanswered text messages and private messages on social media, TJ had continued to call Taylor requesting the money. Taylor cited a broken phone as his reasoning for the unpaid debts and that he would get the money back to him immediately.

'Okay. I'll get it to you soon, mate.'

'I know where you live. I know where your kid lives and I swear I will go and set his house on fire with him and his kids in it if you don't get me my fucking money ASAP.'

'Whatever.' Taylor buttoned the call and attempted to go back to sleep, unbothered by the threats to life.

The End is Near

The week steadied on at a familiar and repetitive pace. Days filled with extreme mood swings from overwhelming sadness to anger, cocaine on tick from a plethora of dealers owed hundreds, and no aspiration of ever paying back said debts. He continued to receive multiple death threats but never cared. 'You will be doing me a favour,' he had responded when TJ requested the money again or would stab him to death.

He had managed to lend £300 from his dad's uncle Mick – he would never pay him back, he already owed him £400 from money borrowed in 2020 for repairs on an illegal motorbike he had at the time – who had been suffering from significant memory problems for the past four years, making Mick a perfect target to feed his addiction. He requested that the money was left behind a wheelie bin because if transferred to his account, his overdraft would have swallowed it up as repayment. Most importantly, he wanted it left behind the bin because he couldn't bear to sit in his company and make small talk.

After a couple of weeks being single, Taylor had felt the most hollow since they split up. An empty soul was the perfect description. He had no knowledge of where Callum was or what he was doing but he could bet all of the money in the world that he was coping better. He imagined that he was out with his friends Ian and that redhead girl he could never remember the name of, or kissing all sorts of new men from dating apps.

The End is Near

Taylor's night terrors had peaked. It was an impossibility to sleep for any longer than 40 minutes without being woke to an empty bed. His heart had begun to palpitate irrationally, his chest growing tight throughout the night until he woke struggling to breathe. The more cocaine he inhaled, the more worryingly his heart palpitated. Over the past five days, it had become extreme. A constant excruciating burn in his chest. He tried aspirin and heartburn medication but neither worked. He had become a hermit and leaving the safety of his flat for medical assistance was not possible. The rhythm of his heart was exhausting because it brought violent pounding from underneath his rib cage.

The end is near.

One Thursday afternoon, Taylor had found a piece of paper on the kitchen counter as he wandered through the flat. It was a letter wrote during one of his coke-infused binges that he couldn't remember drafting. His eyes skimmed perfectly across the letter; failing to acknowledge the terrible spelling and grammar.

To Callum,

Where do I even start with writin this... I'm off my head writin this, off coarse!

The End is Near

I miss you with every beat of my heart. I feel like my life will never be the same now you have gone for good. i hope its not for good but i'm certain it will be if am bein honest!

I need you right now. I just wish you were here to give me a hug and tell me everythin is gonna b ok. TBH, the way we used to be bad on the drugs 6 days a week haha wow that is like a walk in the park to what im doing now. I've sniffed about 50 fucking grams of coke in the past month

My heart feels like it is going to fall out of my chest sometimes but I don't know how to sort it and I don't think it is that bad to go the hozzy over. But it is scary abit... do you think I'm gonna b ok?

I've lost my job for not going in so they sacked me ... they've had enough now. My mum and dad hate me. I'm in debt with about 50 people because iv been lending all sorts to get bits with it

I miss you so so much and Cal i am so so so fuckin sorry for everything what has happened in the past. But now I'm writing this I think it is for myself because you will never see this but I am hoping this could probably take my mind off it. Who knows!

I will love you foreveeerrrr and everrrrrr.

Taylor xxx

Tears dripped onto the paper, his words solidifying the pain and departure. Their home was only his now. Their dreams were only Callum's now. Nothing would ever be the same.

The following day, Taylor snorted five grams of coke and never slept until ten o'clock the next morning. He had succumbed to delirium. The Beatles and Elvis Costello played whilst the summer rain pelted against the windows of the flat, in typical British summertime tradition. The ambience should have been calming but Taylor did nothing except snort drugs, smoke cigarettes, and pace around the flat erratically. He punched the doors until the wood splintered and ripped his fingers open, talked to himself, shouted insults at thin air, and text Callum's inactive phone too many times. It was one of the most uncomfortable Friday nights ever experienced.

The next morning – it was Saturday, although Taylor had no idea what day it was – the first thing noticed was the stench coming from his underarms that made him nauseous. His natural scent had declined recently yet this was peak atrocity. Stale milk with bottom notes of onion. The concept of having a shower and washing his knotted hair as a potential motivator to shift his mood was something he toyed with, which materialised, though to no motivation or mood shift. The introduction to the task took over 35 minutes and three cigarettes later for Taylor to get out from under the cover of his filthy bed and get in the shower. His imagination of how the task would pan out was nothing more than imaginative which he realised when he finished his shower within four minutes and still felt dead inside. The chore was completed in silence with the only noise being the invasive creaking of pipes and droplets from the shower head thudding against the bath floor. He dried his hairy chest and the rest of his body but could still smell dirt, too lazy to shower again.

The afternoon went on with him falling in and out of light sleep whilst obnoxiously bad daytime television – quiz shows and antique auction programmes – played in the background. The comedown from the drugs that Taylor had the night before was plaguing his sleep into a broken one; flashbacks of his relationship with Callum coming to haunt him when he attempted to enter REM. He remembered how he raped him; hit him; mentally abused him, all factors in Taylor's discombobulated sleep. He looked through the empty fridge at potential food to eat but it was hollow and reeked of death. He had lasted until eight o'clock in the evening before having his first line of the day. With cocaine came erratic tendencies. This night led him to call his mother with the hope of mending their broken relationship.

'H-hello. Hello, mum. I was just calling to see how you were getting on. Have you been okay?' he stuttered.

'Do you need more money or something? There's no other reason you'd be phoning me. You aren't getting anything else from me... or your dad, ever again. You still haven't paid us back from last time.'

'Mum, please, don't start. I know I owe you money and I'll give you it back, I promise. I'm just going through stuff at the minute so it's hard but I appreciate you lending me it. Thank you,' Taylor said. An olive branch.

'Don't thank me. I'm the worst mum in the world. I have willingly fed your addiction.'

'Mum, I'm not addicted to anything,' he lied. He could think of multiple things he was addicted to just off the top of his head. Sex. Nicotine. Marijuana. Cocaine. Callum.

'Don't lie to me. I know what you are, Taylor. A fucking cokehead, that's what you are. Just like that twat of a sister I have, Sharon.'

'I'm not, I promise you. It's just because I've lost my job so I have needed a bit of money to get by,' Taylor lied again.

'Taylor, you have been my son for nearly thirty years. Please don't lie to me, mate. One thing I'm not is soft. You should know that. You've had everyone worried sick. I fucking dread to see what that flat of yours looks like. Probably like a fucking bomb has hit it.'

The End is Near

'I'm sorry,' was all Taylor could say.

'I also know that you "borrowed" money off Mick. What an evil person you are. You know that poor man is sick in the head and you took advantage of him.'

'I'm sorry.'

There was a long pause before she grunted, 'I know you are. I know you are, son. You need to look after yourself. It's not fair on everyone else to see you the way you are. I've cried nonstop thinking about you. I get that you have split up but the world doesn't end. You will find someone else, Tay. Just don't go down a dark path. What I will say, from years of experience, son… is that time is the biggest healer.'

Taylor knew from the tone of his mother's voice that she was sad, and likely crying. He reassured her that he was okay, he needed time alone to process his grief.

They spoke and made plans to see each other the following week – if Taylor felt up for it, he said that he would let her know early next week, but it would likely be the day of. His mother buzzed with excitement to see her son again for the first time in months, hoping he would be a different person from the last time that she saw him. The dreaded phone call was not bad when Taylor realised that his mother had his best intentions at the forefront of her mind. He thought that maybe he was right in thinking he was to blame for their relationship falling apart when he was just a teenager. Years of drug taking, encounters with the police, truanting from school, and disrespecting his elders had led to the collapse of their relationship that was once healthy.

Time is the biggest healer.

Time is the biggest healer.

Time is the biggest healer. Her words resonated in his brain like a poetic Shakespearean soliloquy.

There was a deplorable connection between depression and substance abuse; the inability to process feelings of melancholy without retreating to cocaine. No matter how much he told himself that tomorrow was a new day, filled with new opportunities, he always returned to aiding his depression with drugs and liquor.

An idea had sprung in his mind during one of his heavy binges, crucial to the possibility of another future with Callum. Something he should have thought of weeks ago.

He threw a pair of shorts on and headed outside for the first time in over a week. He felt the fine summer rain on his legs as he made his way down the street to a place he would never usually visit. A place where he felt unwanted, disliked, and critiqued.

'Taylor?' Wendy answered the door in her pyjamas with a look of confusion on her face. 'It's one o'clock in the morning. What's going on? Has something happened to Callum? Is he dead?'

'Wendy. Have you heard from Callum?'

'No. Not for ages. I was wondering where he was. Is he not at home with you?'

'He left me, again. But this time I'm actually not sure why he did but that doesn't matter. I need to speak to him.'

'Sorry. I have text him and got no answer,' Wendy admitted.

'Me too, I just want to speak to him. I need him, Wendy, I know you hate me for what I've done to him but I need him so much and I don't know how to get in contact with him.'

'I don't hate you, love. I haven't heard from him. I'm surprised he hasn't messaged to be honest. Or popped down. Do you want to come in for a drink?'

'No, don't worry, I'm sorry if I woke you up. I'm a nightmare. Goodnight, Wend,' Taylor waved goodbye and sprinted back to the block, up the stairs, and locked himself in the flat, before he bawled his eyes out.

He had been erased from his life.

There was no concept of him ever returning.

The end is near.

Taylor stayed awake for three straight days after he visited Wendy at her house, his body fuelled on cocaine. He knew his body was giving up on him, too exhausted to even make it to the toilet without urinating in his pants. His heart palpitated every minute of the day, his lungs slowly caved inwards preventing him from catching a successful breath without maximum effort.

He had another heaped line of cocaine before he attempted to sleep again, unaware that would be his final. The sheet of the bed was damp with sweat as he turned over in the bed to try and find a comfortable position to fall asleep in. When he grabbed his chest, his rib cage felt like it was closing in on his heart. And it was.

'Callum,' was his final word before he closed his eyes for the last time.

The End is Near

The End is Near

CHAPTER ELEVEN

Callum

'Optimistic' young man's suicide sends shockwaves across the city

By **Abigail Cradles** | Weekend Reporter

A promising young man has sadly taken his own life following the devastating news of his ex-boyfriend's tragic passing reported last week.

Callum Jones, age 23, originally from Aigburth, was found dead in his flat following reports of missed calls from a friend.

Callum had left his ex-boyfriend, Taylor Stewart, who died age 29, following a row. The news of his death by an accidental drug overdose had sent him over the edge, the Liverpool Echo has been told.

In a statement made later to the police Ian Murphy, his friend and manager of the local hostel Helpful Hand Initiative in the city centre, said: *'I arrived at his flat following many missed calls not being answered. I know where he worked so I called his work who told me that he had not been in since Wednesday. I was aware of the death of Taylor and I knew he would not cope well with it. My heart is broken, he was the nicest person I had ever met who deserved nothing but the world.'*

His grandmother, Agnes Jones of Aigburth, had also made a statement to the police: *'We had a broken relationship since he met that lad [Taylor], but he was my grandson and I adored him for whom he was. I cannot believe he is gone.'*

A note was found at the scene that is currently with the police as evidence.

Mental Health and Suicide Support

Samaritans: 116 123

Childline: 0800 1111

PAPYRUS: 0800 068 41 41

CALL Mental Health Helpline for Wales: 0800 132 737

The End is Near

To whoever may find this,

Please know that this decision wasn't an easy one but I think that this is the most selfless decision I could ever make. We are all to pass at some point, and mine happens to be now. Please don't remember me in sadness or that this was a cry for help, it was a cry for happiness. My time on Earth has come to an end at age 23 and I couldn't be happier with what I have experienced.

I need to be with him.

You're probably wondering why did I do this? How could I have left the possibility of a happy ending? This is my happy ending. I have lived my life to the fullest and have experienced everything that I wanted. Happiness, sadness, redemption, growth, love, heartbreak, family, friends, sex, drugs, alcohol. This is all there is to life and I have loved it all, but I don't want to experience these things anymore.

I can't believe he's gone. When his mum told me that he had been so depressed, I couldn't possibly live with that guilt.

I miss him so much and I've missed him every day since I packed my stuff and left, again. I wish I never. I've never regretted something so much in all of my life. I thought I needed space but I needed him.

The End is Near

I'm crying so hard whilst writing this. The memories engraved in my mind forever, even when I pass on. I'm sorry that I wasn't the best person I could be. The fact I broke his heart breaks mine. I held against him things that I should never have. We all make mistakes, just as I have. But he treated me like a prince in the end and I hurt him for no reason. I can't possibly forgive myself for this. It would be too selfish.

Thank you to all of my family and friends for appreciating and loving me for who I am – despite of all of my flaws.

To Taylor; thank you for being the best life partner I could ever imagine. You taught me to appreciate myself and I couldn't thank you enough for what you have done to me.

To my nanna; I'm sorry I couldn't have mended our relationship. Thank you for rescuing me from things young children shouldn't see.

Thank you all. I can't wait to reunite up there.

Callum x

The End is Near

The End is Near

ACKNOWLEDGEMENTS

Thank you to all of my family and friends for putting up with me for the past three years rambling on about whether I should write this book and then whether to publish it. The first draft sat in my notes for nearly two years and I have finally decided to take the plunge, so thank you.

Thanks to anybody who decides to purchase this book and read it, I hope you enjoy it. Thanks to anybody who enjoys the book and thanks to anybody who dislikes the book – I am always always always open to constructive criticism!

If you would like to follow me on social media or contact me about The End is Near, you can contact me here:

Instagram: https://www.instagram.com/connorsthinking

X: https://www.x.com/connorsthinking

TikTok: https://www.tiktok.com/connorsthinking

Printed in Dunstable, United Kingdom